COMING UP ON THE SHOW..

The travails of a news trainee

COMING UP ON THE SHOW..

The travails of a news trainee

Shweta Ganesh Kumar

Srishti
PUBLISHERS & DISTRIBUTORS

Srishti Publishers & Distributors
N-16, C. R. Park
New Delhi 110 019
srishtipublishers@gmail.com

First published by Srishti Publishers & Distributors in 2011

Typeset in AGaramond 11pt. by Suresh Kumar Sharma at Srishti

Printed and bound in India

Acknowledgements and Dedication

It's surreal to actually be typing out a dedications and acknowledgement page, for that means that my manuscript has been transformed into a book and that it is now in the hands of you, the reader who has decided to give it a shot. And so, first of all, I thank you for giving me a chance to take you through 'The travails of a news Trainee', the first in the 'Coming Up On The Show' series.

I thank Srishti Publishers for putting their faith in my writing and liking it enough to bring it to a bookstore near you.

I dedicate this book to my 'Appoopan' who took his last breath doing what he always loved, writing. Without him I would have never recognized the power of words.

And also to my parents for their unconditional belief in whatever I chose to do- be it participating in a beauty pageant or courting arrest while campaigning for the environment.

And finally Sagar my husband, for holding me close during the highs and closer during the lows. Without him this book would still be wandering around in the recesses of my imagination.

Thank you all.

Shweta Ganesh Kumar

Prologue

Curtain Raiser

The sound of the TV came loud and clear through all the other sounds.

'So who's in the safe zone this week... Who's the one whose cut makes the cut?' the anchor announced to the apartment it was a part of, the apartment which had the unappreciative audience of one.

'Cut makes the cut! My God! Who on earth is writing your lines? Who the hell is paying you to be a TV host! It's high time someone reviewed the stuff we're watching on TV. Wonder why no one talks about the viewer's rights in this country!'

Satya muttered as she moved the cardboard boxes around, half empty. The idyllic setting of her apartment contrasted with the near pandemonium inside. The apartment in question was a two-room unit with a kitchen and veranda, on the third floor of a house where the landlord stayed on the ground floor. The house was one among fifty-three in a residential colony in NOIDA.

There was nothing striking about the colony. It was what you usually saw in the suburbia anywhere in India. Villa style houses built next to each other, overlooking a plush garden in the middle. Sleepy security guards manned the three gates to the colony, barely looking at the vehicles and people that passed through. Also marking his unobtrusive presence was a gardener who wrapped a large red towel on his head, which half obscured his face as he tended to the colony garden. There was also the necessary evil gang of twelve maids who worked in the houses in the colony, fiercely protecting their territory from the influx of others who came looking for jobs. Yet another constant feature in the colony was a vegetable seller, who was supposed to have descended from a family who had sold their vegetables only in this colony. Gopal *Kaka* as he was known, did not seem to possess a watch, but the colony residents could always set their watch by his long drawn out calls of, '*Tamaaatarr le lo, Aalu le lo*...' He always passed their houses at the same time.

Satya knew that he cycled past her house with his basket of vegetables at one in the afternoon. Today she could hear Gopal *Kaka*'s hoarse call faintly in the distance. She looked at her watch and threw up her hands in exasperation. She was way behind schedule. Dressed in her most comfortable jeans and a warm T-shirt, she stood with her hands on her hips, surveying her flat.

Her well-used corduroy jacket was wrapped around the back of a plastic chair. The plastic table had been dismantled and now lay inside its cardboard packaging. Her trusty old laptop switched off and cold due to inactivity was placed on the chair. The mattress had been stripped off the bed that now served as a stand for two wide open, worn out Delsey suitcases. The steel *almirah* was gaping open and empty, seemingly bereft of the clothes and accessories that it had housed till a while ago. The kitchen was now bare, and the only indicator that food had once been cooked there, was the pungent yet very Indian smell of ginger garlic paste that lingered in the air, long after the last packets had been doled out to the covetous maid. The maid had also laid claim to the soap, the half used shampoo, the rugs and colourful throws that Satya had liberally thrown around the apartment. She had even carried away the shoes that had been a size too small and had an embarrassing squeak when used on wet surfaces. The landlord had promised that he would adopt the remainder of the eight potted plants that Satya had accumulated on the front veranda. They had been part of her own personal "green your surroundings" campaign. Unfortunately she had never had much of a green thumb, or any other green finger. Three of the plants had wilted in the winter due to frostbite and the pots now remained as a memory of the plants that had once made them their home. These too would go to the landlord after Satya left. Gardening was one thing Satya decided she would not be trying out again soon.

She paced around the apartment with her arms full of an assortment of clothes, knick-knacks and utensils, depositing them in appropriately labelled boxes while continuing in her self-designated role as the voice of the disgruntled television viewer. The show host of indeterminate gender, dressed in the tight purple suit, however, seemed to be unmindful of her sometimes critical and often caustic statements. He or she droned on in a high-pitched voice.

'Sorry, Marie your cut did not make it. You're this weeks' split end. Goodbye!'

Satya who had paused in her pacing, drawn by sheer force of habitual reality show watching, let out a deep breath.

'Ohhhh. Why Marie! I thought she was pretty good at the styling! Uff, oh! Here, I go again! My God! I should really stop watching these shows. Both international as well as their desi spin-offs! And while I'm making statements like that, I might as well pledge to be a wonderful human being who will be the first to set foot on Venus. Get a grip, Satya! Who am I kidding? Giving up reality shows it seems…come to think of it, the TV needs to be in its carton before the movers get here! I really need to stop waiting till the last minute to do it! And maybe, in the spirit of stopping things, I should stop talking to myself while I'm at it! Oh damn!'

Almost tripping over the gaping cardboard boxes kept in a row,

Satya reached for her phone, which was currently ringing loudly to the tune of '*Rang De Basanti*'. She had quite liked the rebellious spirit of the movie. And this was the longest she had gone without changing her ring tone. This was uncharacteristic of Satya who not only always knew the latest and greatest in Bollywood but also the not so great. Yet Bollywood was far away from her mind as she blinked to clear the sudden film of pain that had clouded her vision. Her toe had taken a hit. Pressing down on the stubbed toe to ease the pain, she answered the phone.

'Ouch! Hallo, yes? *Haanji*, this is Satya! Yes that's right! Sharma*ji*?'

Satya had to strain to hear Sharma's usually hearty voice. Now that she thought of it, the last time Sharma had been all bubbly with infectious energy was when he had been trying to convince her that his 'Packers and Movers business' were the best not just in the country but the whole world.

'We could even send things safely to the moon madam*ji*!' he had tried to convince her.

Satya remembered that he had said that just after she had signed the agreement. It had not been as reassuring as he had probably hoped she would be. Today, she could hear the loud honking of big vehicles, which she assumed to be trucks and the loud clattering of things, which sounded like crates being thrown around and dropped. This was not a particularly encouraging thing to hear when one is talking to one's packers and movers.

'Satya*ji*, there is a slight delay.' said Sharma's heavily accented voice on the other end. His voice had none of the heartiness of the first time. Satya was losing her patience.

'What do you mean by delay, Sharma*ji*? When is the truck reaching here? This stuff has to reach Bangalore... I was supposed to have you people here by 10:30 am! It's 12:30 pm now! Hallo?'

Sharma*ji* seemed to have been stunned into silence by the cold anger that she had projected from the other side. She waited for a response. After a minute, Sharma cleared his throat and replied, 'Ummm... Oh... *Haanji Haanji*! What time you are asking *na*? One minute hold'

Now she could hear him yelling out in a combination of Hindi and Punjabi to the people who were making the noise, asking them how long it would take. After a lot of combined yelling and mutterings and a few more crashing sounds, he came back on the line.

'Madam*ji*, Satya*ji*, It will take one more hour please. Only one more hour.'

Satya wanted to yell, but settled for a resentful tone instead. She had to trust these people with her belongings after all.

'What, one more hour? Sharma*ji*, you do understand that I have a house to vacate and a flight to catch! And we did sign a contract! Anyway, please be here as soon as possible. I need to send these crates away and vacate the house before I can leave to catch my flight. Thanks a lot and *Namaste*!'

She hung up and resisted the urge to fling her phone at the wall in frustration. Instead she placed it on the table with extreme care. It would not do to have a non-functioning phone at the moment. She tugged at a strand of her hair to relieve her irritation at her schedule being thrown haywire. With an exasperated expression straightening her mouth into a grim line, Satya turned away from the cardboard mountain and headed to the balcony for a breath of fresh air. The TV was still blaring in the background. A nasal voice was asking viewers to stay tuned as the channel had the "Celebrity Apprentice" coming up after the break.

Satya shook her head slightly to clear it and took in a deep calming breath. There was a slight nip in the air that served as a reminder to the bitter winter that had just wrapped Delhi and its neighbourhood in a tight embrace. The colony gardener was rolling up the watering hose after his arduous task of drenching every shrub and flowering plant in the neighbourhood park. A group of pigeons had alighted on the cable lines crisscrossing the area and were cooing loudly to each other much like the gossipy ladies who had daily gab sessions in the park. They had been the bane of her existence for a while, these pigeons. Two of them had made a nest right on her kitchen window and had made it a point to kick up a ruckus as if screaming "Bloody murder", each time Satya went into the kitchen. It was only when all the eggs had hatched and the kids having flown the coop, literally, that the parent pigeons had let her use her kitchen in peace.

Staring at the well-manicured community garden in front of her, Satya barely heard the noisy pigeons. Her thoughts went back to the year that had passed her by. So much had happened. As a reality show addict, Satya used to think that there was no way in which a person's life could be as weird as that of a reality show participant. Yet thinking back of the year gone by, she felt like she needed to revise her notions. The TV news industry had made sure of that. The industry had accepted her, embraced her and then shaken her notions up completely. It seemed like every month had had a special challenge of its own for her to overcome.

Come to think of it, she recalled that it was on this very day, the previous year that she had moved into this apartment. From one February to yet another February, it had been a long twelve months this time. To use a popular cliché, life had indeed been a roller coaster ride. But then most of the times she had felt like she was out on the edge of a precipice, hanging on for dear life. And towards the end of it, she had felt like she had let go and jumped. But fortunately, it was as if the story of her life had been attached to the jumping end of a bungee rope. At the end of the day, the mind numbing fear, the blood curdling screams and the hair-raising jump had been worth it.

Satya smiled at the mental image. It made her think of the superhero comic book heroines who were always dangling from some skyscraper or the other, thanks to the villains who were using them as bait. Only in her case, the larger than life villain was life itself and she had had to rescue herself from all the situations that she had found herself in. Satya wrapped her arms around herself, unwilling to walk away from the veranda just yet. She took in the idyllic calm around her. It was weird how she had managed to lead the life she had had, while living in an environment like this. All around her were families with school going children, clean Maruti cars and kitchen vents which frequently gave out wafts of *Dal* and *Rotis* being made for happy families. For her neighbours, Satya knew she had been the picture of success. She had even seen mothers pointing her out to their daughters as she haggled with the vegetable seller or jogged in the colony park. For them, she was the single, pretty girl who was working in a national television news network, living alone, presumably making loads of money and living the glamorous life everyone in the TV industry did. Right?

Well, Satya knew she would love to pretend that, that was indeed the truth. But for someone whose waking hours had been dominated by a news channel, someone whose only social life was hanging around in the office canteen and being the owner of a salary account, which bordered on the empty by the end of every month, Satya knew that nothing could be further from the truth. And on most weeknights when she had shovelled Chinese takeaway as late night dinners, she had fantasies about leading a routine life. A life in which you could get to the goals you had for yourself by taking a fairly straight route with no twists and turns. A life in which one did not have to feel that giving up ones dreams was preferable to the frustration one went through in making them come true.

'My life has been like a frikking reality show! Straight out of TV…' she thought, 'Everyday… Everyday it's like there were these huge insurmountable tasks I had to get past to stay in the game! Was the prize worth it?' she wondered.

As she stared at the garden in front of her, mostly unseeing, perhaps, like in all good reality shows, it is time for a recap.

—365 days ago—

1

WELCOME TO THE LUCKY FEW WHO MADE IT OVER ALL THE OTHER WANNABE CONTESTANTS!

Satya preened as she put a brush to her shiny shoulder length hair. She practised her camera smile in front of the bathroom mirror. She did not have a full-length mirror yet. As she brushed her hair, she was also standing on tiptoe to check if her outfit for her first day at work was ok. She had bought a designer cotton *salwar kameez* in a sober red shade for the momentous occasion of joining the ranks of the employed. She had had to dip into her meagre savings quite a bit for it, but it was worth it. It had been an agonising decision. Western formals or semi-formals? Indian formals or semi-formals? The one thing that she had been sure about was that her jeans would not have felt right for her first day at the best news channel in the country. That would not send across the right message.

And Satya was very concerned about first impressions. She had always been known as a pretty girl with her big eyes and beautiful smile. But she was always prickly when people misjudged her as just another pretty face. Today she was working hard to create a professional impression and not just that of a girl fresh out of college. Her *kajal* was already in place and all she needed, was for her hair to look reasonably good. But the Delhi heat had not been kind to her already unmanageable locks, making the simple task of putting a comb through them a major challenge. As she wrestled with the frizz, her thoughts went back to the insanity that the past week had been.

Finding out that the office was not technically in Delhi had been a shocker! It was only on arrival, that a hard core South Indian like Satya had figured that the office was in NOIDA which till recently was not even considered part of the national capital. She had been in for quite a rude awakening. Noida was like you were almost in the capital of the sub-continent, but not quite! So one thinks that they are headed to the land, which was immortalised in the 'City of Djinns' and as the 'power capital', and home to many architectural wonders and then Wham! You end up in NOIDA, whose real identity seems to have been sugar-coated for those who end up in the city by mistake.

'Delhi?' the bewildered visitor asks, and NOIDA turns back with an apologetic smile and goes 'Umm! No, but you're close. This is the national capital region!' And that was exactly what hit Satya when she set foot on the dusty soil of the said region and realised that finding an apartment had suddenly taken top priority.

Most auto rickshaw guys in NOIDA behaved as if Delhi was in the next continent while their counterparts in Delhi tried to charge you for the ride to NOIDA, as if they were taking you to Never-

Never Land. The city buses were far and few in between. The ones that you did manage to clamber onto were filled with rude conductors who insisted on being paid in change, lecherous men both young and old, skilled pickpockets and the not so skilled ones, women with impossibly huge shopping bags filled with things seemed to be designed to gouge one's eye out and drivers who were both honk as well as brake happy. Set the above scenario to pitiful ancient audiocassette renditions of men who are caterwauling in an assortment of Punjabi and Hindi, about being dumped by their long-time sweethearts. These were the public transportation options for those who could only afford autos and buses. After one week of such eventful rides, from her temporary residence at a relative's place, Satya was ready to commit either suicide or homicide. And so her natural inclination was to find an apartment as close to her workplace as soon as possible.

Now as she brushed the last tangles of her stubborn hair into behaving, her apartment doorbell burst into insistent peals with her cell phone starting off too, a mere 10 seconds later. The sudden noise startled Satya, who overbalanced from the tiptoe pose she was standing on.

'Ow!' she cried as she stubbed her toe. It was the second toe of her right foot as usual. She had always had a propensity to stub it. Right from childhood, she had wondered many a time, why it was always that particular toe. She had many memories of answering phones with a ten second delay thanks to the sharp pain from the hurting toe. You would think that she would have got used to it by now, but sadly the pain was still as strong as it had been the first time. Sadly musing about the toe, she hobbled slowly across to the table, where her ringing and vibrating phone was now doing a horizontal jig on the table.

'That's just great! A ringing doorbell and a ringing phone! If I were in the shower as well, the picture of chaos here would have been complete! God! Am I supposed to be some ancient goddess with fifteen hands or something! How am I supposed to attend to all these things at one go?'

She yelled out in complete annoyance. Choosing the phone over the doorbell, Satya pressed the answer button with one finger as she continued to try and wrestle her hair into submission with the brush.

'Dude, why aren't you opening the door? And you also took a long time to answer the phone,' went a slightly accented patronising voice. Satya knew only one person who could sound patronising and whiny at the same time.

'Rehaan, how on earth did you know that my doorbell's ringing? Oh! Let me guess! You are the brilliant soul that's holding onto it like it's the end of the world and my doorbell will save you from certain death! And if that was not enough, you decide to call me up at the same time as well! What is wrong with you?' she shrieked.

The bell suddenly stopped as if the offending finger that had been pushing it had dropped off the visitor's hand. Rehaan's clipped terse voice rang through the phone.

'There's no need to be nasty, Tya! I was just making sure that we are on time on our first day at the office! You said 8:30 am and its 8:35 am, the rickshaw guy is waiting here and if you don't get down soon, we'll have to pay him five more rupees!'

At this point the voice had taken on a plaintive tone. A mental image of Rehaan's pale but handsome face drooping flashed in front of Satya's eyes. She smiled despite herself. The occasional whininess and annoying behaviour not withstanding, he was her best friend after all. And not to incur the wrath of a plaintive best friend on the first day of a first job, Satya quickly responded.

'Ok, ok *baba*! I will be there before the water works start! Give me two minutes ok?'

And with that she hung up and dropped the comb on the floor of the already cluttered two-room apartment. She looked at the comb as it joined her half-unpacked suitcase and damp bath towel on the floor.

'Oh well, not like *Amma* is here to yell about tidiness,' she thought with a mental smile and a twinge of homesickness at the memory of her mother and all things familiar and comfortable. Picking up her well-used sling bag and locking the door behind her, she ran down three flights from her terrace apartment. Flushed from the run downstairs, Satya slowed down to pat both of her landlord's dogs on the head. After a neat skip over the puddle of pee that the older and more obese one had made, Satya was at the gate. Her smile widened at the sight of her best friend who was waiting for her.

It was always Rehaan's slightly oversized nose that caught one's eye first and then the rest of him. Wispy hair neatly combed across a square head, with a cloud of strong men's deodorant hanging over him, Rehaan was standing there, looking ridiculously pompous in a formal shirt and trousers. His expression would not have looked completely amiss on a puppy dog. His hand was still resting next to her apartment doorbell by the main gate. Satya's wide smile did not seem to help in getting Rehaan's cheery self back. So Satya decided to try another tack.

'Drop it Rehaan! I am here now right? Can we get going now please?' Satya asked with a hint of a plea in her voice.

'It's our first day after all! The day we dreamt of in college! We are finally part of the broadcasting industry…' she continued. At which point Rehaan cut in.

'And the rickshaw guy's waiting too… You wouldn't have change on you right?'

She swung around and gave him an incredulous look. Rehaan's tendency to be short of cash and borrow almost all the time had been nothing short of a legend when they were in college. She was used to doling out money but she had also always kept the strictest of accounts. However, Satya had assumed that he would now make an attempt to change his ways considering that he would now be making his own money. Apparently, that was not to be. But Satya decided she was going to take a stand.

'What! No way! You are not doing this! So this is why you insisted on picking me up! And here I was thinking what a wonderful friend! See how he's come to pick me up! And now I see its only because you want me to pay for the rickshaw! And by the way, you still owe me money from the Mc Donald's lunch before the farewell!'

Satya huffily declared as she clambered onto the rickshaw struggling to keep her new *salwar kameez* as crease-free as possible. Rehaan climbed alongside with a wounded expression on his face and gestured to the rickshaw guy to start moving. He shook his head from side to side in a melodramatic fashion.

'You are so petty, Satya! That was like ages ago. And this after I help you with your apartment, tell the landlord about the upcoming journalist that you are, nag him to reduce your water charges…this is what I get in return.' He ended with a heavy sigh. Satya rolled her eyes and then turned to look at her 'drama queen' of a friend. She patted him on the hand.

'Ok, ok! Quit whining and stop getting senti on me! I will pay the rickshaw guy today and you are a wonderful person, blah, blah, blah! But this is the last time okay.' Satya said, with her eyes on the road, trying to focus on what her first day was going to be like. Though seemingly placated by Satya's quick response, Rehaan was still on the topic. He was still muttering away going, '…the pages of classifieds, the really shitty one room places through the dingy alleys, the over the top expensive cupboards trying to pass themselves off as houses.'

Satya was drawn into remembering the house hunt, despite herself. She started off too.

'Not to mention the slimy brokers! Ugh! Creepy! This was the forty first place, remember?' Satya said, reminiscently.

It was true. The search had been long and difficult. They had pored over yellow pages, grey pages, pink pages and every other coloured page they could get their hands on. When they found an apartment they liked, the reasons the landlord or landlady found for refusing them were many.

"Oh, She's single!"

"Oh, she's in the media! You people keep bad hours and have bad morals!"

"She cannot have any male guests, including father, brother and cousins. They must wait on the road and meet her outside."

"You can only cook vegetarian food."

"You should become a vegetarian."

And so on and so forth. The apartment, which she had finally chosen, had not been the prettiest one they had seen in the course of their search. But the landlord had been by far the best. Good old Mister Malhotra. And his two friendly dogs, both of which were fat. One was bordering on obesity and seemingly serious heart disease. With no ridiculous rules or prejudices, Mr. Malhotra or Malhotra Uncle as he insisted they call him, also had friends amongst the media and his only condition was that the rent was to be paid on time. Satya had signed the contract with a sigh of relief. And now she was starting to fall in love with the apartment that was the first place, that was truly her own. Thinking about the search, she was grateful that she had Rehaan by her side when she traipsed around NOIDA hunting for a suitable place to stay.

Lapsing into silence, they continued. Rehaan who had checked out the route the previous day, told her it would take around fifteen minutes from her sector to the one where the office was located. Satya decided to put the time to good use by soaking up the sights and her first impressions of NOIDA. It would come in handy when she was writing her memoirs as a famous TV journalist, she thought to herself, smiling as she did.

The roads were wide and separated by hedges that acted as dividers. There were cows of every conceivable colour on both sides of the road. Most of the cows were grazing, unconcerned by the vehicles that whizzed past them, while there were a few lying down with their long limbs gracefully crossed beneath them. Then there were the adventurous calves that were trying to cross the roads, mustering all their courage to do so. Satya grinned at the sight of one particular calf putting a hoof out on the road as if it was testing the waters. She felt like she could identify with the calf as she was on her way to test the waters at her new job too. Putting a hand to her cold nose, and enjoying the feel of the morning breeze on her hair, Satya smiled to herself thinking she could probably fall in love with the city that was not a city. The thought had not fully sunk in yet, when a Maruti 800 filled with loud throbbing music passed by. And in the car as well as hanging out of it, was a bunch of guys who were yelling lewd remarks in pure Hindi. Taken aback at the other side of NOIDA, Satya wrinkled her nose in distaste.

'Well, maybe its not time to fall in love just yet,' Satya hastily thought.

However no amount of loud yelling by dim-witted youth could quell her anticipation of officially being a part of the broadcast industry. She and Rehaan were two of a batch of thirty-five that had specialized in journalism for their masters degree. When they had started on the course in a mass communications institute, two years ago, there had been just one established English news channel in the country - the Nation Today or the NT network. One could either become a part of the NT network or daydream about being a T.V reporter while working for a newspaper or a magazine. This was of course, the sole private English news channel in the country.

The only other option for broadcast wannabes was the government owned India twenty-four. Though India twenty-four boasted of the most modern equipment and technology, the old stereotype that applied to government jobs could be applied here as well. You work hard till you get a government job and once you land the job, you hardly work. That's what happened to most journalists who took up jobs at India twenty-four. Most of them relied on the seasonal interns to do most of the work while they relaxed in their air-conditioned offices. Nation Today plucked the ones who refused to let their spirit die and continued to work. Those who stayed on at India twenty-four would get promoted purely by the years they spent there and not by the quality of work they put in. What was worse was how most reporters there were forced to change their political loyalties in accordance with the political party that was ruling the country at the time! India twenty-four did not have much space for a man or woman who had, what was called a spine or an opinion of one's own.

What with only India twenty-four and Nation Today to choose from, it seemed as if there were not many enticing prospects for young TV journalism graduates. Yet as if the congregated aspirations of wannabe T.V journalists everywhere had set wheels into motion, the past eight months had seen two new English news channels get launched. And peaking television news ratings within the first six months of its launch, Nandan Bhave's N.E.W.S India had quickly stepped on NT Network's toes. Of course, India twenty-four could not even term itself competition. The only viewership it had was in the far reaches of the country, where cable television was yet to percolate and in households where paying for television was akin to selling your soul to the devil.

Satya could still remember the thrill of getting to know that N.E.W.S India would be coming down to her institute for placements. Everyone in her batch was ready with the local stories they had broken or reported in the college newspaper. The college news bulletin tapes were re-edited to be shown to these prospective employers while everyone practised their best T.V smile. In the days before the interview, the college corridors rang with unusually grammatically correct sentences delivered in deep and formal voices instead of the usual "Wassups" and "Hey dudes". Even those of Satya's batch mates who had believed in the power of print and had looked down upon the frivolous nature of TV journalism were slowly but surely being drawn. Maybe it was the money associated with the industry, maybe it was the reach to illiterate regions of the country, something newspapers could not manage. Or maybe it was just for the sheer but simple high of seeing yourself on TV and calling up your folks to say, "Look Mum! I'm on TV."

Satya remembered the rush she had felt as the panel from N.E.W.S India had questioned her about the kind of reporting she wanted to do and the difference she would bring to the TV journalism scene. She had almost passed out because of nervous energy, the day before the interview results were announced.

Jolting her out of her reverie, the cycle rickshaw came to a rumbling halt in front of a tall glass and concrete structure. Her first impression of the building was that it was indeed imposing. However, there was no board anywhere to indicate that they were truly at the headquarters of what was reported to be the "most watched English news channel in the country". Probably to keep the fame hungry lunatics of the nation from descending on the channel with their resumes and homemade videos, Satya concluded. From the other side of the road lined with scraggly trees, Satya saw Tina and Shanks jumping off another rickshaw. They completed the group that had been picked up by the N.E.W.S India network. While Satya and Rehaan had been close friends from the first week of college, they had never really hung out with Tina and Shanks back then. This was the first time they would be spending time in such close quarters with the duo.

While Satya fumbled for change, she could see Tina approach them from the corner of her eye. Replete with her horn-rimmed glasses and dressed in her trademark *kurta* and jeans, she had her sneakers on as well. Tina seemed ready for her first official day as a TV journalist. However, Shanks or Shankar Subramaniam as his parents had named him had not bothered to change out of his oversized t-shirt and sinfully low jeans.

'I think he's still chewing gum,' Satya whispered to Rehaan before Tina caught up with them.

'Allo, so we've made it on time. What say we inaugurate our first day by heading off to the canteen?'

Tina trilled in unnaturally cheerful tones. Rehaan acknowledged her suggestion with a nod and then ambled over to Shanks who seemed to be hunting for change to pay the cycle rickshaw man. Satya nodding her agreement too and looking at the office building with an intense gaze, said 'This is surreal. After all those interviews and mock bulletins and real assignments, we are here! This is it... N.E.W.S India, we've got every direction covered!'

2

SO YOU THINK YOU CAN BE A JOURNALIST?

One coffee and two oily *dosas* later, a helpful guard ushered the group into the bustling newsroom, which was the heart of N.E.W.S India. After the perky little yellow coloured canteen that gave out waves of warmth despite the slightly weird smells inside, the group was taken aback by the futuristic style the rest of the building had. Done up in the channel colours of red and blue, there was serious business written all over it. As if to drill in the point, a close look revealed that the word 'news' was painted in continuous lines in all the corners of the walls.

Satya ran a slightly nervous hand over the 'news' painted on the walls. She figured that the interior designer had probably been overwhelmed by the idea of working for N.E.W.S India and therefore ended up including elements, which were not really required. She knew how being overwhelmed felt like. They were not yet in the newsroom and already her palms were getting a tad sweaty and her breath was catching, not to mention her heart that seemed to be doing disco moves inside her chest. She focused on her surroundings again. Apart from impressing on everyone that they were in the business of news, the network also seemed to guard its news quite seriously. There were at least three security guards on each floor and one needed shiny access cards to be let into the actual floors from the elevator lobbies. Satya and her friends were already impressed and the tour had not even started yet.

Gleaming edit suites lined the corridors, which the four walked through to get to Cabin B. They had been informed by their placement coordinator that this was where their new boss would be. Cabin B was the lair of senior news editor, Mr. Ram Kedia. Walking by faces made familiar from daily news bulletins and quite a lot of unknown but glamorous ones, Satya and the others slowly advanced towards Kedia's cabin. All four had interned with news organizations before, so quite a lot of the sights were technically not all that different. Yet it was as if the momentousness of the occasion had dumbfounded them. Even Shanks who had walked around college with a 'nothing can faze me' expression was looking suitably chastened and awed by the behind the scenes action.

Satya found herself looking at every chair and every computer she passed with respect and a weird sense of ownership. This was what was used to sift through and screen the massive amounts of information that came in to the channel. It was through these machines that the news passed through before reaching thousands of viewers. And now she too was part of this huge news-generating beast.

From now, she too would be wielding a microphone and battling the weather conditions of rural India to bring to the nation's viewers the real state of the poor, the facts behind the villages with no water or electricity, reports on government schools with missing teachers and the like. Neither rains nor riots would stand in her way. Her dream was within grasping distance.

Being a TV reporter had been Satya's goal ever since she had stepped into high school. She had aced her English literature exams and gone on to become the editor of her pre-university and university newspaper. During her masters, she had learnt to operate the camera and shoot her own stories. And each time she used the college edit suite and saw herself doing her sign-off on the monitor, she knew that this was what she wanted to do with every pore of her body. She knew that there was nothing else that would make her happier than reporting the news as and when it happened. Today, she was minutes away from beginning to realize this goal of hers. Each step Satya took towards Kedia's cabin was a step towards her dream.

She glanced across at her friends. They all seemed to be lost in their own thoughts. All of them were walking in step to an unheard rhythm, waiting for the moment when the rest of their life began. This was the day they had spent sleepless nights for. In companionable silence that was tinged with a dash of tension they walked on. But before they reached Kedia's cabin, the unexpected happened. The group stopped in their tracks. Satya gaped unashamedly. She had never in her wildest dreams thought that she would run into the charismatic owner of N.E.W.S India on her first day there. But there he was - tall, smiling and with a weather beaten face - the face that was a nightmare for the nation's greasy politicians and also one that inspired a thousand idealistic aspiring journalists. Twenty-five years of journalism experience as well as all possible kinds of awards and accolades at the age of forty-four, walking in their general direction, in flesh and blood was Nandan Bhave.

Nandan was supposed to have started off as an economics student, with no journalistic background whatsoever. Unemployed and with a flair for writing, he was said to have wandered off into the Indian State, one of India's oldest newspapers offices. It was from there his career kick-started. Starting off as a cub reporter, he had risen to the ranks of a senior political correspondent in eight short years. He had also dabbled in news documentaries on his own. When in his twenty-fifth year in the industry, he had decided to launch a news channel. Critics had almost completely panned him. But with eight months of topping the rating charts and enough profits to consider launching a Hindi news channel, Nandan's work had silenced all the critics quite thoroughly.

Satya could feel her jaw drop and palms begin to get moist with nerves as one of India's most celebrated journalists of all time headed in their general direction. Busy issuing instructions on the phone, Nandan stopped mid-conversation and looked at the foursome. A wide smile splitting across his seasoned face, he said, '*Oye*! You guys are the new uns! Welcome aboard! Met Ram yet?'

The question being aimed at no one in particular threw the group off-balance. They all wanted to answer, but they were all dumbstruck with awe. Just as Satya felt her tongue untie itself from the multiple knots it had tied itself into, she heard Tina jump to the forefront. Her confident, slightly gruff voice rang out loud and clear.

'No Sir, but we're headed towards his office.'

'Good, good! Come meet me if you have any issues,' he said in his deep voice before he turned back to the phone and walked away. The four kept watching his retreating back as he moved away and walked out of the newsroom. Tina turned to the group with a smug smile, which said it all. Satya felt like kicking herself for not speaking up to her idol. Rehaan and Shanks on both sides of her looked suitably crestfallen as well.

'I'm going to make this up to myself. I am going to be such a fine reporter that Nandan will have my number on speed dial,' she thought. She repeated the thought to herself, as they continued on their way.

The group could feel several pairs of eyes scan them as they walked past the different desks to Kedia's office. Some of them stopped talking as they passed by. Satya noticed that most of the people on the desks were of their age group. The newsroom looked like there were very few people who were past their mid-thirties. But then, most of the experienced journalists would have their own cabins, she reasoned. She wasn't very comfortable with the way people were looking at them from head to toe. It reminded her of the first day on campus, when seniors looked at freshers as potential targets for ragging. Satya was sure that she even noticed a couple of girls eyeing Rehaan with interest. She turned to look at him, to see if he had noticed. But he seemed to be lost in his own thoughts, presumably upset about missing out on the chance to speak to his idol too. Satya also saw a guy looking straight at her and trying to make eye contact and smile. Satya resolutely looked the other way. Sure, the guy was cute. Most people in the industry were if not attractive, at least well groomed. They were all either on-air already or attempting to be. Looking polished was one of the job specifications. Satya could not afford to get distracted by those types right now. One had to keep focus. This was her first day in the office and she did not want to be distracted by anyone or anything.

The energy levels in the office seemed to be at dizzying heights. Satya could barely hear herself think over the combination of loud murmurs and distinct yelling that seemed to have become a separate news dialect of its own. There were sets of TV screens poised atop tall pillars that were set throughout the newsroom. Each TV was set to a different channel- both national and international and in some cases what seemed to be a live feed coming in from different locations. That probably explained the loud yells of, 'Ravi, did you see that the BBC has a ticker running on Mumbai, why don't we have that news confirmed yet?' or 'Who's monitoring the feed from Screen 16? The mob seems to have gotten violent there.'

There were purposeful looking people who were running across the rooms with mini DV tapes. There were people unmindful of the chaos, with the scripts of their reports in hand, practising their voice-overs as they waited for the voice-over rooms to get free. Someone seemed to be shooting an Internet based report in a corner of the newsroom. The reporter was trying to get the people around her to pipe down a bit as she attempted to shoot her piece to camera or the PTC as it is popularly called. Observing the sights in the newsroom was like flipping through a handbook on the basics of TV journalism at one go. From shooting and reporting to editing and telecasting, the room encompassed it all. It was also fun to just stand and indulge in the art of people watching. The dressing styles ranged from the formal news anchor style to the torn jeans and flip-flops.

'No way, Shanks would be feeling out of place here,' Satya thought, 'Some of these people look like his fashion soul mates.'

Making their way through the bustling newsroom, the group finally reached Cabin B. They exchanged a quick look with each other and smoothed down their outfits and their hair. Well, all of them except for Shanks who looked around for a dustbin to deposit his gum. Satya had once told Rehaan, that she was pretty sure Shanks was born making his chewing the cud expression. He had never been seen with a set of still jaws. After Shanks managed to find a dustbin, the gang was officially ready to meet their new boss. Taking the initiative, Rehaan stepped forward and tentatively knocked on the glass door. The door opened and holding onto the handle, they found themselves face to face with the formidable Ram Kedia.

Average height with greying hair, a slightly blemished face, eyes that were eerily expressionless and yellowish teeth - there was really nothing that screamed T.V journalist about Ram Kedia. His clothes were non descript and he seemed to be the anti-thesis of the stereotype of the T.V journalist. There was no charming smile nor was there an outstretched welcoming hand. On the contrary, he seemed to be glowering at the lot of them. It was not a very encouraging reaction to get on the gang's first day in office. But Kedia did not seem like the kind of guy who was worried about the kind of impression that he was leaving on them.

Kedia was rumoured to have latched onto Nandan about five years ago, after fifteen years of being a failure as a print journalist. He had never made an appearance on screen though and it was not hard to imagine why after meeting the man. Though never seen before and heard off only after the public relations machinery for the channel had kicked in, after the launch, he had suddenly been made out to be a force to reckon with in the industry. How and why this was so was never asked or mentioned. He had made a reputation for himself as a fierce news editor in the broadcast industry. Though one of Satya's seniors who had interned with NEWS India had told her that this was probably because he was known for being extremely short tempered and unreasonably so. A couple of tabloids had splashed a few pictures of him dancing with a glass of whiskey atop his head at an industry party. Yet the very next day, the story had been killed. And neither he nor the channel was ever asked any embarrassing questions about the incident. When someone was a friend of Nandan's, no one questioned his or her credentials or the number of pegs they had gulped down before losing control and sanity. This was Ram Kedia, the man who was alleged to control quite a lot of what N.E.W.S India's viewers saw or did not see on-air. In a channel that insisted that all employees were to be on a first name basis with each other regardless of their grade, Kedia was the only one who preferred to be known as 'Ram Sir'. This was the man who Satya and her friends were designated to meet, the man who from this moment onward was responsible for what would happen to them in their new roles as employees of N.E.W.S India.

'So you're the new bunch, eh? Want to be journalists, eh? This is the right place! O.K! So you know your stuff, eh?'

He suddenly spoke in a burst. His voice was guttural and his speech pattern neurotic. He also seemed shifty-eyed because even though the dialogue was directed at the gang, he was not looking at anyone in particular when he spouted the words, which were interspersed with the "Ehs". Suppressing the urge to say "Eh" right back at him, Satya decided to take the opportunity to speak up.

'Yes Sir,' she said in response to his query. Taking a look at the three others who were nodding in assent at her lead, she went on.

'We've been trained in camera handling, shooting, scripting, reporting basics and anchoring.'

Finishing with what she thought was a T.V friendly smile Satya noticed that instead of looking happy at acquiring a new batch of trained, diligent reporters, Kedia's face now had a dark scowl.

'Eh?' he demanded, 'But that's reporting stuff. You are all in production. What have they taught you people in production basics, eh?'

Satya was too taken aback to respond. Though she did open her mouth to reply, she soon found out that the only sound that escaped from it was a gasp. Rehaan came to her rescue and cut across the stunned silence.

'Sir… But we are here to be reporters, not to be in production. That's what we've been trained to do. I want to cover politics. Satya wants to work on development stories… And, and …'

Kedia silenced him with a malevolent glare and busied himself by looking at a printout in front of him. He sputtered on as if Rehaan had not spoken.

'Hmmm… So that's great eh! You go and recruit journalism school graduates only to learn that they are good for nothing. Now, I have to schedule an editing workshop for you. Hmph. Who comes to become production trainees without editing training, eh! Anyway, so who's Rehaan Khan? You're with the business team. Report to Varghese. Shankar Subramaniam goes with sports. Tina Aggrawal and Satyabhama Menon go to the general news desk. You two will report to Padma. All clear eh? Now go meet the HR persons and complete the formalities, eh?'

With that Kedia gestured them to move on with his hand and then turned away and strode on in what seemed to be the short-legged imitation of Nandan's stride. He was obviously done with whatever little time he had set up to welcome N.E.W.S India's latest employees.

Dumbfounded as they were, the gang instinctively moved away from cabin B. Kedia's little speech had left them feeling like they had been dealt with body blows. Satya got a sudden vision of dark clouds gathering over what was supposed to be her sunny little walk to the TV news hall of fame.

'It's probably just a little road block,' she tried to convince herself desperately. She had dreamt of this for too long to give up so soon. So she would have to do production for a while, so what? She was part of a news channel now and how long would it take for her to switch to reporting anyway.

'Not long!' she thought to herself. But it seemed like N.E.W.S. India had other plans for her. As Satya and the gang walked towards the exit to head to the Human Resources department, she could hear the people by Kedia's cabin start discussing them. They were commenting on how professional they looked despite being so young. There was no time to let the compliments soothe the freshly created official wounds though, as Kedia had hastened to belittle them. From behind their haze of shattered dreams, they heard Kedia exclaim disdainfully.

'They thought they would be on T.V eh? Silly children. Not even twenty-three and walk in wanting to be Nandan. They thought they could be T.V reporters, eh!'

Trying hard to keep the disappointment from showing in her stride, Satya kept walking.

3

THE APPRENTICE

TRRRRINGG!!!

The alarm on Satya's mobile phone went off. Set to sound exactly like a traditional alarm, the phone had always done its job admirably well. Waking her in time before every exam in college and making sure she had never missed a train, Satya had always depended on her phone before. However Satya did not seem to need its services anymore. Well, at least she had not for the past two and a half months. Drenched in sweat, with tendrils of damp hair sticking to her forehead and cheeks, Satya reached over and hit the snooze button. She had been lying awake anyway. It was 11 am and though she did not have to go to work till 3 pm, it was impossible to sleep.

The city itself was caught up in the throes of the sluggish but tight grip of the dreaded Delhi summer. Satya felt like she was as much a victim as the next person. And having an apartment on the topmost floor certainly did not help. It was as if she was living in a pressure cooker, the only difference being pressure cookers had an outlet and her apartment did not. And it was not just the heat that was turning Satya into an insomniac. The experiences of the past three months had done their fair share too.

The Human Resources formalities had gone on fairly well, till the group had received their new designation.

'So your designation is News Trainee,' the stout little man from HR had read out in an indifferent voice. The four who received the news however, were indignant to put it lightly. They had exchanged incredulous looks at his little announcement

'But what is this supposed to mean? It's like no-man's land or an odd - jobs - boy designation. It's not like trainee reporter or trainee producer or something... trainee something!'

Rehaan had burst out in fury. He was right. He was also by far the one that was most affected by the news. Rehaan was the only one in his family who had rejected the traditional professions of medicine and engineering to take up a career which virtually no one had opted for before him. The only other person in his family who had had anything to do with the media had been an uncle who religiously wrote letters to the editor every week. And not all of them had gotten published even. Back home in Rehaan's town in Kashmir, he knew he would not be regarded with a lot of respect with a designation like that. It seemed to him that all his dreams of handing out a flashy visiting card with an important sounding designation was dissipating in front of his eyes. Who would believe that he was on his way to become a respected TV reporter when he said 'Hi I'm Rehaan Khan, news trainee'

It just did not seem right. The designation seemed like a fuzzy title of someone who was training for something that was vaguely related to the news industry. Satya shared his sentiments. But her reasons were very different from his. Her family was full of print journalists and writers who had urged her to follow in their footsteps. She had sought to prove them wrong by opting for a different medium of journalism. And now far from being on-air metaphorically waving a triumphant microphone in her relatives' faces, she was stuck with a designation that meant nothing.

'It's not even a designation. How am I supposed to tell people that this is what I do? How do I explain my profile to people?'

Satya had wailed over the telephone to her parents as soon as she had reached home. The human resources department was frankly not very concerned with what the news trainees of their organisation felt about their designation. They had important things like their own lunch breaks to get back to. Though a human resources department is essentially put in place to look after the welfare of the human resources of the company, the people who worked here seemed to have no such compunctions. They had waited for the group to put their signatures on the employment forms and other formalities and then dropped yet another bombshell. They added to the group's woes by casually mentioning that the designation would stay put, indefinitely. So now they were news trainees till the company deemed fit. And god knew how long that would be.

It was a dejected group that reported for work the next day. They had met up with batch mates of theirs who had previously been envious of the N.E.W.S India team, as they were now known, for being employed by the network. But now on hearing of their vague designations, the envious looks had transformed into looks full of pity. After dinner, the four of them had decided that they would not be organising or attending another batch dinner for a while. In the newsroom now, after woeful looks at each other, they had set off for their respective desks.

Satya and Tina were to report to Padma Govind, the head of the general news desk. Forty-six year old Padma Govind was an established name in the behind the scenes world of news production. Starting her career at India twenty-four, she had moved to Nation Today in a few years. She had quit Nation Today as senior news editor, made three award-winning documentaries and then joined N.E.W.S India. Newsroom rumour said that Padma had never lost her temper, but also that she was known for her keen news sense and her hawk like gaze, which took in every detail. Dressed in a pair of worn-out jeans and an old T-shirt, Padma looked up from the monitor as the duo approached. With a swift movement, she moved her glasses to the top of her greying head. Running an impatient hand through her short wiry looking hair, Padma looked them over. Though the scrutiny was brief, Satya felt as if she had missed nothing. There was probably some truth to the rumours after all.

'Oh yes, the new kids. Satyabhama and Tina is it? Welcome to the N.E.W.S India network. So we'll have a weeklong edit workshop for you first. As Ram tells me you need to learn the ropes. And after that you start working at the desk. We deal with all the general news, as you know. That includes reports from all our bureaus on politics, crime, city etc. All the other news like entertainment, sports and the like will go to the respective desks. You'll get a hang of it soon enough' she said in a low-pitched but pleasant voice.

She smiled at them and turned her attention back to her monitor. She obviously thought they would move on now that she had finished giving them instructions. Satya who did not see a point in staying on made to move, but Tina tugged at her hand and hovered around. She cleared her throat and then started off.

'Ma'am when do we get to move to reporting?' Tina asked with what was obviously an ingratiating and hopeful smile. Padma who had put her glasses back on, propped them back on her head again and gave Tina a cool gaze.

'Two things my dear girl,' she said without the slightest change in her tone, 'One, no one calls anyone Ma'am or Sir here. We use each other's names. And two who ever said you could move to reporting? I do not remember any such indication being given to you by our recruiting team. Yes, I agree that you were recruited by N.E.W.S. India, but we never said you were being taken in as reporters, did we? Now please find our video editor Sarath for your edit workshop. He should be in one of the edit suites at the further end of the newsroom'

She had put her spectacles back on in a dismissive manner and gotten back to her work. Satya did not know what had chilled her more, the fact that Padma had seemed scary even without the slightest change in her tone or the finality that she had heard in Padma's response. The duo had walked away in silence. And very soon Satya had seen her life adapt itself to a new working schedule. Not that she liked it, but she lived through it helpless as the days whizzed past her. And somewhere in between the insomnia had snuck up on her.

The sunlight was filtering in through the thin cotton curtains at Satya's apartment and poking at her like hot iron rods. Though her eyes were still tightly shut, Satya could make out that the day was disgustingly hot and sunny, from the angry reddish shade her eyelids seemed to be. They continued to be red despite her clamping her eyes together and squeezing them to blot out the sun. She gave up, realising that beating the sun in Delhi summers was next to impossible. The sheets were sticking to her clammy skin.

'A cold shower is in order,' she thought and slowly sat up in bed. The fan was radiating hot wafts of air and only served in plunging her mood to further depths. It was bad enough to be doing something that she did not want to do. But having to go in to work to do just that, and that too at three in the afternoon on a full-fledged Delhi summer day was worse. Even the idea of lying in bed till the worst passed over was not tempting. The bed seemed to be sending out heat waves, as if the mattress could not bear the thought of contact with another being in this extreme heat.

Satya was yet to invest in an air conditioner or a cooler and the frequent power cuts made her think that it would be a bad idea in any case. She had been resorting to putting dripping wet towels over herself before going to bed. But then most of the time she had woken up in the middle of the night to peel off a dry or sticky towel off her body. Today, she guessed she had peeled off the towel at some point during the early hours of the day, when she had fallen into an exhausted sleep. She spotted the towel lying at the foot of the bed. She felt sluggish. But she could not just continue sitting there. It seemed like there was nothing else to do, but push herself off the bed and prepare for the rest of the day. As Satya forced herself to get off the bed to head for a shower, she knew that the prospect of what lay ahead was not an appetising one.

The shift she was on was the afternoon shift that started around 3:00 pm. However the term 'afternoon' shift was a misnomer as it went on till 11:30 pm. A typical news day is divided into three different shifts – a morning shift, an afternoon shift and the most hated of them all, the graveyard shift. A morning shift was typically from 7 am to 3 pm. And the graveyard shift from 11:30 pm till 7am or whenever the people in the morning shift decided to come in after having oily breakfasts at the office canteen.

These shifts however do not bind the senior news editors. They come in to work around 11:30 am to noon and leave by 10:30 to 11 pm. But they do not have to follow the timings rigidly. On slow news days, they are free to come in at a time best suited to them, to have leisurely lunch breaks and leave long before the 10 'o' clock news bulletins. It's everyone else associated with the production of the news that have to follow the strict scheduling of the shifts.

Most morning shows are a rehash of the best news reports from the previous night. On an average news day, as opposed to a day slated to have a big news report or a day where breaking news suddenly happens, the flow of the news is in a fairly orderly manner. The news flow picks up by around 11 am and then steps up as the hour passes. By the time the poor afternoon shifters walk in, the flow has become incessant and furious. From the unreasonable wrath of the news editors who have been on slow boil since the news flow started, to the fury of the news that has been gushing in from all quarters- this is what the fate of a person on the afternoon shift looks like.

The prime time bulletins of every news channel are telecast from 7pm to 11pm. This is when every news-watching eyeball is hooked onto their favourite news channel. And every person working on the afternoon shift is primed to keep those eyeballs focused there and if possible pry a few from the other rival news channels as well.

The first thing that Satya had learnt on the shift was that the number of people on each shift was inversely proportional to the amount of work. And this meant that the afternoon shift was perpetually understaffed. As a news trainee, Satya was one of the people that made sure that the bulletins had enough material and more, to run for the half an hour spot they were telecast on. Each shift had a team called the desk editors who took the first look at all the information that poured in.

N.E.W.S India had twenty-four bureaus across the country and not all of them had edit machines or voice recording suites. Some of them were just basic two-member teams with a reporter and a cameraperson. The resultant footage from this combination of reporting and shooting is sent to the headquarters in NOIDA via satellite. Now imagine a total of nineteen bureaus without production personnel and only reporters and camerapersons gathering the news. Next, visualise an average of three teams per bureau working on at least three different stories per day on an average day. And finally, picture at least three streams of footage pouring in from each of the nineteen bureaus. And simultaneously streaming in, are the emails with the scripts of the news reports- some good ones, some half-baked ones and some that seem like you would need a codex to solve the cryptic clues to get to the information in them.

This is the barrage of information, which the desk editor has to confront every shift of every day. Once they make the scripts readable or 'cleaned up' in desk editor lingo, the shots in the footage are shortlisted to go with every sentence in the script. Then the script goes to a copy editor who 're-cleans' it before it is handed over to a voice approved desk editor. This lucky person would then record the script or do the voice over and then edit the story to the rhythm of the voice over. The fully edited story would have a maximum duration of one and a half minutes, with every shot having to last for at least three seconds. Less than that and the viewer would not be able to register the shots in the report. However just because a desk editor spends four hours scripting and editing the perfect story, there is no guarantee that it goes on air. The rundown editors who choose the stories for their shows take that decision. And the ultimate 'Yes' or 'No' was always in the hands of Padma and her fellow heads of the news desk, Chetan Roy and Aneesh Ramnath.

So where did Satya and her friends fit in, in this newsroom

hierarchy? They were right at the bottom of the food chain. They had started off as shadows to specific desk editors who were seniors and had designations, but only by dint of having joined a month before Satya and her friends. A month before the channel's HR had canonised their procedures, especially those of designations. It was just a matter of bad timing. For Satya, the duties of a shadow had meant running to the feed room to see if her desk editor's assigned footage was incoming or waiting behind an edit machine till it was free so that she could call her desk editor trainer - Aniket Varma.

Aniket had lorded over her to his hearts content. He seemed to treat her more like a minion than a person he was supposed to be training, to become a desk editor like him. While he did show her the ropes around certain software and short cuts on the edit suites, he never missed an opportunity to rub in his seniority. He also made it a point to frequently emphasise the fact that her designation meant nothing. Apart from delegating her work from his load, he also made her call logistics for his office drops and generally pretended she was his personal assistant. The worst of all the duties had been the frequent trips to the coffee machine to get Aniket his hourly dose.

Having someone else's coffee cup in her hand while she should have ideally been holding a microphone did nothing for Satya's confidence and spirit. It also did not help to be called 'junior' for the sole reason that placement week in their college had been a week later than placement week in Aniket's college. Though the shadow duty was slated for two weeks, every minute had seemed to stretch on seemingly defying all known laws of time and physics. Finally after two weeks of shadow duty, the gang had been put in different shifts with the same duties as desk editors. A week ago, Satya had completed two and a half months in the afternoon shift.

'The smallest cog in a great big news wheel, that's all that I am. Go through the motions of postproduction for someone else's story. Stuck behind the scenes, while some others get to live the life that I've dreamt off…' Satya thought as she finished getting ready. The shower had been boiling hot and she wished she could apply Burnol instead of her daily moisturizer. There were definite disadvantages of having an apartment perched on a terrace. Shoulders drooping and with a dejected expression, she locked the door behind her. Reeling from the heat wave that engulfed her, she quickly walked to the staircase. Now she would have to stand around in the sun looking for a cycle rickshaw guy. Weirdly enough, staying out in the sun seemed preferable to the task that she had in front of her. Not only did she have to drag her unwilling self to office, she also had one of the most dreaded of all the desk duties today- that of manning the ticker!

4

MISSION TICKER

The air-conditioned comfort inside her office did nothing to bring back Satya's dimpled smile. The fifteen-minute rickshaw ride in the scorching sun seemed like an omen for the day ahead. The red Rexene cover of the rickshaw seat had been scorching and there had been gaping holes on it as well. Each time the rickshaw guy had braked or turned a corner rather sharply Satya had put a hand on the seat to steady herself and ended up burning it on the wire mesh that poked from underneath. She made a mental note to buy Burnol. It seemed like she needed it for more reasons than one.

But then again for Satya, the agony of the ride was nothing when as compared to her assigned work for the day. She was on ticker duty – the innocuous looking news worm that scrolled at the bottom had the dubious distinction of claiming one victim per shift. The person responsible for the ticker usually collapsed due to the amount of news that had to be fed to it. This especially held true during a breaking news situation, which meant that there would be a constant stream of news flashes and updates. And everything on the ticker had to be triple checked for accuracy and spelling. It was the instant news solution for many a viewer who liked to get their daily dose of news as they jumped from channel to channel. And though they did not have the time to spend watching an actual bulletin, there were some who actually took time out to mail in, reporting the spelling mistakes they saw on the ticker and how it was a shame that a national channel like N.E.W.S India could get a spelling wrong. For the viewers it was just a mail, for the person on whose shift the error was reported, it meant a public dressing down and sometimes, even worse.

With a sense of foreboding, Satya took her seat in front of the ticker machine, which was essentially a desktop computer, which would only have the ticker software and certain news feeds running on it. One could only open office mail on the ticker computer. You could not open any of your personal mail sites or even Google to pass your time. Social networking sites were banned as well. The ticker area was one to be approached with utmost seriousness and complete dedication. Feeling much like a monk, who was about to enter her zone of total isolation and complete meditation, Satya readied herself for the task at hand. She would be taking over from Rati who had moved her swivel chair to the side to make space for her. As soon as she had caught a glimpse of Satya, she had buried her face in her hands in a gesture of absolute desperation. After pressing her fingers to her eyes briefly, she looked up at Satya.

'I thought you would never come,' Rati wailed. Plump with long hair cascading down to her shoulders, Rati Iyengar's normally pleasant face was crumpled up in distress. She had been manning the ticker for the morning shift and by the looks of it things had not gone well.

'It's been a horrible day, Satya! A four-year-old child falls into a fifteen-foot ditch in Punjab, late last night. We've been getting updates every twenty minutes. And I've not even been able to get up for lunch. It's been eight hours of 'Jarnail's still breathing', 'Jarnail's let out a feeble cry', 'Fire-fighters reach the spot'... I mean, I'm sorry for poor little Jarnail, but do we have to give our viewers 'blow by blow' accounts! It is a tragic situation, yes I completely agree! But it's not a national security issue or something! And on top of that I've not been able to move from here for even a second thanks to the flashes. And you were supposed to be in by 3 pm. You are late!' Rati ended on a high-pitched shriek.

Squishing down the urge to yell, in front of Rati's genuinely exhausted face, Satya took a deep breath. She had come to know Rati reasonably well over the last two and a half months and she liked her. She knew that it took a lot to shake even-tempered Rati out of her constant state of pleasantness. Rati was the kind who went out of her way to be kind to others. Satya mentally shuddered at the thought of the shift that Rati must have gone through to end up in this kind of a state. She leaned over and gave Rati a quick hug.

'But I'm here now, right? And it's only ten minutes past three. My mistake I dawdled over lunch. Plus it's not like I really wanted to come in, in the first place. You know *na*?' she said.

Rati smiled back with visible effort and replied, 'Yes I know, I know. I'm sorry woman. I didn't mean to go off like that… It's just the hunger and stress getting to me. Anyway I knew I was handing over to you *na*, so I've just updated the politics, sports and nation tabs. You'll just need to take a look at international in like twenty minutes or so. I thought you might need some time to get acclimatised after coming in from the heat and all.'

Satya smiled at her friend as she shook her head and took a deep breath to get ready for ticker duty.

'See this is why you're the sweetest person ever Rati, I wish we were in the same shift,' Satya said, meaning it with all her heart. Rati was one of the few genuinely friendly persons she had met at N.E.W.S India so far. They had become friends after the "Tape Dragon" episode.

A month into the job, Satya had found herself face to face, with the one of the foremost of a desk editor's pet peeves, the mail from the tape library. Like most other news channels, N.E.W.S India too had a vast tape library that was a source of stock shots of every personality that had graced television news, human or otherwise. The library also filed away all news reports that had been telecast on N.E.W.S India. More often than not, desk editors had to check out tapes from the library to source footage for reports that did not have enough.

Satya had had to fall back on the library when she was editing an obituary report or an Obit as it was called in the newsroom, of a renowned Shehnai maestro. She had checked out a number of tapes from the library for footage of his concerts as well as shots of him hobnobbing with the dignitaries. After a long shift, she had delivered the tapes back to a gangly boy who was manning the tape register. The next day she had walked in to a curt mail with the subject 'Pending tapes'. The mail went on to detail that she had not returned six stock tapes and now had to pay the library one hundred and fifty rupees per tape. Satya had stared disbelievingly at the mail and even gulped down a few choice swear words. It was a quite annoyed Satya that had stomped back to the tape library.

'I'm going to give that what's his name a piece of my mind,' she had furiously thought to herself. However destiny had other plans for her, as it had consistently proven since she had become a N.E.W.S India employee. As she walked into the tape library, she came face to face with someone who was popularly known as the "Tape Dragon".

Glowering eyes fixed her with a baleful stare and silenced her with a single glare. It was C.K.P, the dragon who possessively looked after the tape library. At four and a half feet, with scraggly hair combed across his scalp that shone through, he ranked high in the desk editor's list of recurring nightmares. They tried to avoid stepping into the library when he was prowling around. Somehow he seemed to believe that people borrowed tapes for mischief and sent them dire threatening messages about misplacing tapes whenever he deemed fit. It was the female desk editors that more often than not seemed to be the targets of his wrath.

'Was he a woman hater?' Satya thought as she gulped and slowly advanced forward.

'Ummm, I came because…'

'You, you are the girl who has to pay one hundred and fifty rupees per tape. You have lost six tapes!'

He spoke in a deep voice filled with bitter foreboding. Satya managed to gather her courage and spoke up, 'C.K.P, ummm I mean Sir, that's the thing... I did return them. Yesterday evening!'

'Oh, so why isn't your signature there in the register?' he asked with a mean glint in his eyes.

'Cos I wasn't asked to sign anywhere...he asked me to leave the tapes in the basket and I did!' Satya replied frantically.

'Who did? Did I? Who did?' C.K.P asked aggressively, with the air of a spider that recognised a victim when he saw one. Satya went blank. She did not know the name of the gangly guy. She opened her mouth and then shut it, willing her blank mind to respond with a name, any name. C.K.P's eyes were glittering now.

'Sooo... You people do not even bother to know the people who painstakingly organise the footage for you. We are just low lives, aren't we? People who toil for the likes of you! Do you even know what my real name is? And like that wasn't enough, you go and lose tapes like its personal property! What do you people think of yourself? And are we not people that are worthy of being known? Just because you strut around the newsroom, you are superior you think?'

He was ranting. Satya was not sure what his issue was though, whether it was the fact that she seemed to have misplaced tapes or the fact that she had not extended a hand of friendship to those who dwelled in the tape library. She silently berated herself for never asking him his full name or that of the gangly boy's for that matter. She would have mutely continued to listen had not it been for his next threat.

'I have increased the misplaced tape fee to 200 now! That means you have to pay me 1200 rupees! Right now!'

He finished with a look of sadistic pleasure. Satya felt her heart stop. It was the end of the month and she was already on the verge of penury. There was no way she could cough up that much and that too for tapes she was sure she had returned. She shook her head in dismay and was about to start her plea when a voice behind her came to her rescue.

'C.K.P why haven't you logged these tapes that are lying in the out basket?'

Satya turned to see Rati who was idly looking at the tapes in the basket. She rushed towards her and all but snatched a tape from her hand. It was one of the so-called missing tapes. She turned to look at the dragon who had turned red-faced.

'Why are you poking your nose here? I'll have to check if you have any unreturned tapes also.'

C.K.P sputtered. He seemed to have lost all the bluster that he had, had a moment ago. Meanwhile Satya pulled out all six tapes from the basket and placed them with a slight thud on the table in front of him.

'Can I go now?' She asked in icy tones. He nodded looking deflated. Rati put her arm on Satya's shoulder as they walked out.

'You ok? The dragon can be quite scary at times!' She asked.

Satya smiled back. 'Ya, I'm Ok now! Though I didn't understand what his issue was! He seemed to be as pissed at me for not knowing the library staff's name as for supposedly misplacing the tapes! What is his full name anyway?' She asked in a mystified tone.

Rati giggled and said, 'God knows! Not like he's pally with any one of us, for us to know! But you relax ok? All that drama was 'cos he has a crush on you!'

'What!' Satya exclaimed as she stopped dead in her tracks.

'Yup, he's done the same routine with Lini, one of the desk editors here! You know her *na*? He knows it's the end of the month and that we'll be short on cash and all, so in return for waiving off the fee, he'll say that you could maybe discuss it over dinner…' Rati trailed off. Satya looked at Rati incredulously. She smiled at Satya's expression.

'It's true. But he's harmless. He just doesn't have a lot of friends, thanks to his own antics. Anyway Aniket told me that you had stomped off to the library with an upset expression, so I just followed you to check.'

'I'm really glad that you did Rati! Being bankrupt like I am, I would have even agreed to a movie after dinner!' Satya said with a smile.

'Awww! You poor thing! Let me treat you to lunch today!' Rati had replied, giving her shoulder a quick squeeze. And Satya had agreed without much ado.

Satya smiled at the memory of the episode as she focused on the ticker.

'I think the last time we had a meal together was when I was still on shadow duty' Satya said as she scanned through the ticker update pages. While it was O.K for her to have brief conversations while at the ticker desk, keeping her eyes away from the monitor for more than two minutes would earn her a sharp reproof from the copy editor in charge of the shift. The ticker was to be supervised at all times. Especially during breaking news situations where news updates had to be fed in almost within the minute they came in. The person on ticker duty had to be constantly on his or her toes and if not they were brought to book by the copy editor.

Today as luck would have it, the copy editor in charge of the afternoon shift was Debashree Mukherjee. Sharp tongued with a dour face framed by misleading angelic curls, Debashree was known for handing out the meanest comments- well deserved or not. She had left her copy-editing job in a business newspaper for this one, for the sole reason of earning more money. However she made it clear to anyone who asked or did not, about the frivolousness of the broadcast medium, about how it was impossible to report a story in depth in the time span of ninety seconds and much more in a similar vein. And yet, she made no attempt either to change things or to go back to print. She was content with expressing her bitterness at having to let go of her ideals for money, through scolding every subordinate of hers for the slightest mistakes. Today, Debashree seemed to be engrossed in tongue lashing Arvind, another desk editor for what she thought was a badly edited script.

Rati gave Arvind a commiserating look, from behind Debashree's back and continued chatting with Satya. Catching up with Satya seemed to be a good way to pass time as she waited for Aniket to wrap up and join her for lunch. Rati and Aniket had been friends since the first day of work and always hung out together when they were in the same shift. It was Rati who had convinced Satya that Aniket was actually all heart and that the bullying was just his way of becoming friends. Though sceptical at first, Satya was cautiously warming up to him. Aniket seemed to be taking a long time to finish and so Rati figured she had more than enough time to chat with Satya.

'So you've been on this shift for two and a half months now. Usually we get shift changes every two weeks. You must be really good under high stress situations. They must really love you here' Rati remarked.

'Or really hate me,' Satya grimaced.

Rati squeezed her shoulders, threw a quick look at Debashree who seemed engrossed in her work and then turned back to Satya and continued, 'So when do you hang out with your friends and all? They're all in different shifts right? Especially Rehaan! Must be hard for you guys.'

Keeping an eye out for any possible typos in the ticker, Satya distractedly replied, 'Well… I've never been that close with Tina and Shanks anyway, so it's not that bad. And Rehaan and me try to meet up for at least three meals a week and during weekly offs. So that's not all bad either. It's pretty decent actually. It's the work that bothers me more than all of this.'

Rati pressed on, 'But as a couple… isn't that super hard? I mean after being together constantly, now you hardly meet. It's pretty tragic. I mean all of us on the desk keep talking about how you guys look so cute together and now you barely get to meet and it's so sad…'

She trailed off in a melodramatic way. Rati was known for watching every romantic Hindi movie in the theatres. And if she missed them, she hunted out DVDs and watched them over the weekends, or satisfied herself by reading a romantic novel or two. The very core of Rati's romantic being, had been strongly affected when she had heard that Satya and Rehaan were in different shifts.

'What?' Satya exclaimed. Her fingers clashed on the ticker keyboard with force displaying her emotions.

'We're so not a couple. We've never been a couple and never will be! That's the funniest thing I've ever heard,' Satya choked. Rati was taken aback.

'She must be upset 'cos its private', Rati thought. She wanted to slap herself for being so insensitive.

'Oh! I'm sorry Satya! Calm down, I didn't know it was such a sensitive issue! Oh my god, you're crying! I'm so sorry!'

Rati spoke in an urgent yet compassionate undertone as she saw Satya's heaving shoulders. As Satya turned her swivel chair around, away from the ticker machine and with caution thrown to the winds, Rati saw that Satya had tears in her eyes. She had wrapped her arms around herself in a tight embrace. However the emotion was not quite what Rati had expected. Satya was laughing. Her shoulders were heaving in what seemed to be an internal struggle to clamp down on her mirth. Rati was mystified. As she stared at Satya, unsure of what move to make or what to say, Satya burst out, 'I'm sorry, but haven't you guys noticed? I'm not his type!'

Rati continued to look baffled, when Satya grinned and decided to put her out of her misery. She looked at her and simply said, 'He's gay Rati.'

Rati's cheeks flamed indicating how she felt about her huge gaffe. She opened and closed her mouth looking like a goldfish. She looked like she was struggling to find something to say. However before an embarrassed Rati could react, someone else did.

'Satya, why are there two tickers on the ISRO working on the Chandrayaan?'

The voice was full of foreboding and dark, very, very dark. Satya's smile withered at Debashree's reprimand. She swivelled back to the screen and winced. In her excitement, the keys she had accidentally pressed had duplicated one of the ticker items. It was not a monumental disaster, but it certainly was not the smartest thing to have happened either. There were no two ways about it.

Debashree waved Rati away from a red-faced Satya. As Rati apologetically made herself scarce, Debashree came and stood directly behind Satya. She said sternly, 'This is a news organisation. One mistake and you are misleading thousands of people who are watching us. We don't have time for incompetent people like you.'

Debashree finished with a pompous air of finality. Her eyes were glittering with scorn, as she watched Satya squirm under her stern gaze. The unfair judgment rankled. Satya bristled as she struggled to hold onto the reins of her fast flaring temper.

'It's just a repetition Debashree. I'm sorry, but I'm deleting the duplicate and things will be normal ok?'

She quickly deleted the ticker and mentally willed Debashree's temper to return to normal. But her telepathic powers did not seem to be at their best at the moment. Nothing seemed to have the power to stop Debashree from harping on.

'Are you trying to be patronizing Satya? You cannot take things so lightly. How are things right just because you have deleted the duplicated ticker huh? What about the millions of viewers who already saw the duplicated ticker? What about our channel's reputation that has now been compromised because you were manning the tickers? There's a thin line between inaccuracy and duplication. And then you talk to me like that?'

Satya lost it. Her temper flared.

'How am I being patronizing? It was a mistake and I corrected it! It's not like I keyed in that ISRO's found alien life forms on the moon for god's sake. It was a slip, I agree. And I am very sorry. Why are you blowing this out of proportion? It's not like we're the BBC or something. We're just another news channel!'

Satya regretted saying the words as soon they left her lips. Debashree pressed her thin lips so tightly together that they went as pale as her face.

'Oh, so that's what you think is it? If that's the case, then why do you even bother to work here? I'm sure the BBC will be waiting for you with open doors. Why not apply there? This is unacceptable behaviour Satya! I'll have to talk to Padma about your attitude,' she said dourly as she walked away.

Satya remained rooted to the spot. As Debashree stalked away, what struck Satya was how the tiff had scarcely made a ripple in the ever-present chaos of the newsroom. It seemed like the unfairness was routine. By dint of being on the lowest rung of the editorial ladder, Satya should have anticipated and prepared for a disproportionate reprimand.

'Oh well', thought Satya, 'Now that I'm doomed, I might as well go and pack my bags!'

Dejected, she returned to her vigil at the ticker desk. Mechanically she went through the motions of updating the ticker. She looked through Reuters and Associated Press feeds for international one-liners. The occasional news flashes about Jarnail and his predicament in the ditch were handled with extreme care. And though the rest of the shift passed uneventfully, Satya found that she could not gulp down the lump in her throat.

Padma's desk was directly in front of her. And though her back was towards Satya, every time Padma got up or stretched or made the tiniest movement, Satya would catch it. Her heart would then proceed on a slow journey up to her mouth. She would wait for Padma to walk up to her and tell her in no uncertain terms that she was fired. Or sometimes the mental scenario was a bit different, it was Padma beckoning to her with a finger and handing out a letter that had 'Fired' typed out in bold in the middle of the sheet. Scenario after scenario played out in her head as she continued to handle the tickers and wait for her impending doom.

Finally it was 11:30 pm. The end of the shift! The people in the graveyard shift had arrived and it was time to hand over the ticker baton. Satya had started to believe against her natural instincts that the incident would not have a backlash. No one else had mentioned the gaffe. Maybe, just maybe the place was not as unfair as she thought it was. She decided to take a look at her mail before she wrapped up for the day.

'Oh the shift roster has come. Lets see when my weekly offs are…' she thought as she clicked on the message. And there it was printed in red.

'SATYABHAMA MENON ASSIGNED TO THE GRAVEYARD SHIFT TILL FURTHER NOTICE'.

It was more or less the equivalent of a punishment transfer. The words swam in front of Satya's eyes. She felt as if she could hear a death knell tolling in her head.

5

WOES-VILLA

'This is all because of you! All because of you and your sexuality,' Satya growled at Rehaan as she picked at her food. Rehaan and Satya were sitting in her apartment. They were having dinner from the Chinese takeaway they usually ordered from, Dragon Chinese. It was one of those cheap Chinese restaurants that offered the best Indian Chinese possible. Satya swore by it as her comfort food for all reasons and seasons.

N.E.W.S India was blaring in the background on Satya's fourteen-inch TV, which her mother had gifted to her to celebrate her first job. Rehaan had got the food delivered. It was his turn to cheer up his best friend who was obviously down in the dumps. She had been a rock through college when he had first opened up about being gay. She had fought with the idiots who made wisecracks and shunned the straight guys who had acted weird around him. She had even broken up with her boyfriend because he had been disapproving of

Rehaan. Rehaan had never seen anyone as strong or even as stubborn as Satya when she made up her mind. But right now, he was concerned about her.

She had been in the night shift for four weeks now and was in a constant state of whining and high sensitivity. It was like a case of never ending PMS. The cheery, bright girl he had befriended on the first day of college seemed to be getting slowly and surely replaced by a negative, grouchy one. And one with a pessimistic streak as well! Rehaan had thought Satya's favourite Chinese takeaway would cheer her up. But she seemed to be wallowing in self-pity. She was sitting cross-legged on her bed, oblivious even to the fact that, it was the news story that she had edited that was playing on the bulletin. She got through her shifts mechanically and hardly ever spoke of any story she worked on. She also seemed listless more often than not.

As Rehaan leaned back on the wall sitting comfortably on the floor cushion he was sprawling on, he had to admit to himself that he was now seriously worried about Satya. He had thought that she was just having adjustment problems in the beginning. It was not like she was the only one stuck in a bad situation. All four of them had come to NOIDA to become reporters and all four had been slapped with the 'news trainee' tag. Even Rehaan had been seriously affected by the turn of events. It was as if they had all been tied down before they got to start their careers. But he was trying to make the best of the situation, while Satya seemed to be getting more and more depressed day by day. He wondered how to broach the subject. He took a minute as he absentmindedly looked at the next-tomotionless lizard on the ceiling. It was staring at nothing in particular, looking disturbingly like his best friend.

'You don't seriously believe that all this is because of me, right? I mean, you can't blame me for being gay, Tya!'

Rehaan started off mildly. He was careful not to sound too defensive, for fear of setting her off, as she had been prone to, whenever they had this conversation.

'You know that's not what I meant Rehaan.'

Satya responded in a high pitch stressed out voice, which was her tone most of the time now.

'Have I ever been less than supportive of you? Ever? It's just that if I hadn't been so caught up in explaining our relationship to Rati, I wouldn't have pressed down the keys by mistake and that hag wouldn't have gotten a chance to push me into the graveyard shift. Bloody nonsense! I know… I know that, it doesn't seem like a valid reason. But I'm at a stage in my life where I'm just using any excuse to try and justify the crap that is happening right now. I feel like I'm drowning! See the thing is you don't understand how horrible it is to be where I am at right now. It's like I am one of the invisibles that inhabit a parallel universe. I am the hollow woman without any of the entitled fringe benefits. It's not like I get to raid the canteen invisibly or something. I am just INVISIBLE for all practical purposes. I mean think about it! I walk in to work after all the high and mighty ones of our office, have left for their homes. So they do not know or care that a person named Satya works here. I work my fingers to the bone getting things ready for the early morning bulletins. Bulletins which no one ever watches, unless they too are doomed to graveyard shifts like me! And if you were doomed to everlasting night shifts, why the heck would you give a damn about the rest of the world? So how does it matter that I am even working? My team of desk editors is made up of the ones who have either been punished or are too slow or incompetent to work when there are live news bulletins. The technical editors in the night are dead slow too. Its almost as if they couldn't care less about how their editing comes through. Manav Singh, the copy editor on the shift, has requested to be on the night shift perpetually because he's a junkie who can't stand daylight. We have to copy edit our scripts by ourselves again, after he takes a look at them. And then with the constant non-exposure to daylight, its like, we feel ok coming out only after the sun says tata, goodbye. Now I know why it's called the graveyard shift, I feel like I'm one amongst the living dead. Its not like I liked my job either ways, but this is the lowest I can sink Rehaan,' she finished in a despairing voice.

Satya sniffed and it looked like she was trying hard not to cry. It was a losing battle. A lone tear slid down her right eye and plonked onto her bare forearm. Rehaan was not sure of how to respond. He knew that one wrong move would have her completely bursting into tears. Yet he waveringly went ahead.

'Umm... you should just think of your favourite saying you know, the one about it being darkest before dawn,' he said with an earnest expression on his face.

Satya looked up from her Hong Kong fried chicken and rubbed

her eyes with the back of her palm. She gave Rehaan a wry smile. She knew that her friend was trying hard to bring her out of the slump she was in. She felt like she owed it to him to keep her cool or to at least attempt to stop with the tears.

'Well that's my second favourite saying these days Rehaan. My most favourite one right now is, the light at the end of the tunnel is probably the headlights of a train coming your way.'

Rehaan burst out laughing at Satya's droll delivery.

'C'mon Tya! Things will be ok soon, you'll see. This is just a speed bump! And it's not just our work I'm talking about, maybe we'll end up in some nice meaningful relationships this year, you know.'

Rehaan fluttered his eyelashes in a comical way making Satya smile. Rehaan had been looking for the perfect guy for the longest time now. He was known for his unnaturally high standards in a relationship and his bad luck in finding someone as well. He had screened out at least three guys after meeting them for coffee and the one guy who he had reasonably liked had been a Canadian whose visa had expired within a week of meeting him. He had been slated to return, but hadn't gotten in touch after he'd gone for a trek in Nepal. Rehaan's love life was usually taboo. If he had brought it up himself, it surely meant he was on a mission to cheer Satya up and she understood and appreciated the effort. Satya giggled despite herself.

'Ya right! With my current luck I'll probably end up with some knife wielding obsessive psychopath who will find it amusing to cook NOIDA fried Satya. So thanks but no thanks,' she said, making a face at Rehaan as she continued.

'Plus, at the moment I want to concentrate on getting to the other part of news production. I am tired of seeing morons share on-air space with the likes of Nandan or Bhanu who's just superb as the face of the eight 'o' clock news or even Subrato with his sports exclusives! You know what I mean, right? Some of our reporters can barely open their mouth without making a million grammatical and pronunciation goof-ups. And then there are the over confident ones who are hollering out over-dramatic statements of hyperbole. Like the other day, this story about the partial bridge collapse in Hyderabad comes in. Fortunately only four people were fatally injured as opposed to the number potentially having been a lot more if the collapse had happened during the day. Anyway this happened at three in the morning, and so there were only around a couple of cars and a lone drunk cyclist on the bridge at the time. So we were getting footage of Anita Reddy doing a general walk around and description of the scene. She was the night reporter in Hyderabad that day. Whatever she sent us was to play in the morning bulletins, ok? We had no other news from the south. Anyway, so I am looking at the footage, and checking for audio glitches and then I hear what Madam Anita is saying. There she is looking at the camera with a devastated expression going, *"this is one of the worst accidents to have happened in India"*.'

'No way Tya, I can not believe that,' Rehaan cut in, in a tone of total disbelief. Satya got off the bed and placed the plate on the table with a clatter.

'I am not kidding, Rehaan…'

Gesticulating vigorously with her hands, she continued, 'So I am listening to this and thinking, yes that's right, of course all the other accidents like trains falling off bridges, boats and ships sinking, and other human tragedies were all figments of someone's overactive imagination. Of course, it was then up to me, to delete that nonsensical line. And then I started thinking, why is it that I have to be the one editing this piece of absolute garbage to go on air, when I should be out there, covering it with the perspective it deserves!'

Rehaan did not know how to react. But fortunately for him, Satya had meant it as a rhetorical question. She went on, 'It's just worse when I have to clean up after that sort of trash. So that numbskulls like her and worse, end up looking good and well informed, when it's the back end people like us who are putting in all the dirty work... I hate being behind the scenes. And the worst part is that few TV news viewers know that it takes two to three hours to create that minute and a half long clip that they see on their screen! No one knows about the back end workers... about us!' Satya sighed heavily and rather despairingly.

'Anyway... I'm done unloading my tales of woe on you... You tell me, how the business desk is treating you? All well on the money front? Is our economy where it's supposed to be?' she asked in a mock-serious tone.

Rehaan figured that she wanted to change the subject, shrugged in a non-committal fashion and replied, 'Well, it's a long way from the political reporting I wanted to do of course... But it's not that bad. Varghese is heading the desk right? He likes the way I've picked up the nuances of business reporting so he might let me do an actual report of my own, if I come up with a good idea that is. I've been pouring over the pink papers and the not so pink ones looking for some inspiration. So lets' see…'

'Wow, that's good news Rehaan! I'm so happy that things are working out for you,' Satya said with an obvious attempt at enthusiasm. She continued in the same falsely cheerful tone.

'And Tina and Shanks? What about them? I've hardly seen them since my night shifts…not that I missed Tina in any way!'

Rehaan who did not catch the inflection in her voice, licked the Schezuan gravy off his fork and answered, 'They're doing quite well, I think! Tina's still in the morning shift, but she edits quite a lot of reports per day. She keeps bragging about being the fastest desk editor or some such nonsense. You know the way she used to be in college na? Though last time I saw her, she was trying to figure out a way to approach Kedia on shifting to reporting. I'm not sure how that ended. And Shanks, well that's the funniest story Tya! He's officially quit from the running to be India's next top T.V reporter. No more reporting dreams for him! He loves production. He loves the detailing and the virtual anonymity of the job. He told me when I bumped into him at the canteen the other day. I told him, that he also saved himself some money, 'cos otherwise he would have had to ditch his hip-hop look for something way more formal right! Great that he's happy no?'

Satya nodded silently, snatched Rehaan's empty plate and headed in the direction of the kitchen. Dumping the plates into the tiny sink, she proceeded to wash them with unnecessary force. Rehaan sensed that something was amiss and followed her into the kitchen.

'Tya? Are you ok? You'll scrub that plate into oblivion if you keep that up! Quit scrubbing! Are you ok?' he gently asked.

'No, I'm not ok!'

Satya suddenly yelled, slamming the plates into the suds, making quite a splash. The soapy water splattered all over her. However the drenching seemed to drain out her sudden fury. As she turned from the sink wiping her hands on her faded old track pants, she looked like a small girl who had been scolded for playing in a puddle. With soapsuds delicately balancing themselves on a couple of strands of her hair and on the tip of her nose, Satya looked pathetically woebegone.

'I am such a horrible person,' she said in a sad and quiet voice.

'I mean, I should be happy for you, 'cos you're getting the chance to move up from this and to work your way out. You're getting appreciated. And I should be happy for you... and Shanks and Tina... Well maybe not Tina, 'cos I don't like her so much, she's just too bossy and annoying. But you, I should be happy for you, you're my best friend. I just feel envious of you and irritated at my work. I ... I don't know what to do Rehaan...I don't like what I'm turning into.'

As she desolately trailed off, as if on cue her phone started ringing from her bed where it was lying next to the pillow.

'Hallo, *haan*? Ok.'

She hung up and turned to Rehaan.

'That was Samrat from logistics. My pick up is on its way. You better head home. I'll catch you later during the week and will text you tomorrow, ok?'

Rehaan knew that this was not the end of this conversation but he knew that Satya would need time to compose herself before she set off for work. He picked up his satchel and sat down on the chair to wear his sandals. He was not sure what he could say to cheer up his best friend. But he wanted her to know that she would be okay. He looked up from the tiny buckles and said, 'You know this is going to pass, right? What you are feeling is normal…it doesn't make you a horrible person or a bad friend! Just human! We all go through it from time to time! I'm here for you Tya!'

Satya smiled at her friend as he finished adjusting his sandals.

'I know Rehaan. Thanks dude! Now scram! If I'm not waiting by the gate in ten minutes, my cab will leave without me! And I need to finish locking up and cleaning up before that. And thanks a lot for the dinner,' she paused and then playfully added, 'For a change!'

Relieved at her slight change in mood, Rehaan gave Satya a quick hug.

'Ya, Ya! I send money home, unlike you spoilt brat who gets a TV as a gift!' he teased back.

'I'll run now and don't forget to text if you have something to say or just randomly also. Goodnight Tya! Have a nice day or … night rather! Tata'

Satya tugged at his hand as he stepped out.

'Dude, one minute, I forgot to ask and I've been wanting to forever! You were supposed to tell your mother right? Did you? Like does she know you're gay?'

Rehaan stopped mid way and turned and made a wry face at her.

'Not yet! But I think she knows something's up. Back home we get engaged young na, so she keeps sending me photographs of these girls and I keep rejecting them. And now she suspects I'm seeing someone here. She doesn't know how far from truth she is!'

He grinned at Satya's disapproving face and before she could retort, he strode off.

Satya changed quickly from her oversized t-shirt and tracks to a comfortable t-shirt and a fresh pair of jeans and sneakers. The one thing she liked about the night shift was that she could dress comfortably without worrying about having to impress the big shots. It's not like they would be around to observe and take note. Scrunching her hair up into a ponytail, Satya picked up her handbag and locked up. As she reached the gate, she could see headlights from a vehicle flood the sleepy road, announcing its arrival. It was a Tata Sumo, her office cab. She jumped in to join an assortment of N.E.W.S India employees from different departments. There was no one from the general desk today. Though she vaguely recognized Varsha from the online department, she was not close enough to her to strike up a conversation. Settling for a smile of acknowledgement, Satya settled down to peer out of the window for the rest of the ride.

NOIDA looked almost sinister at night. At 11:15 pm there were hardly any vehicles on the road. But then again, it was not like the city was known for its happening nightlife anyway. Most of the cycle rickshaw pullers were stretched out on their rickshaws. There were groups huddled around a low bonfire, which looked more like it was for the light than the warmth, during those balmy summer nights. Every huddle also had a tea seller handing out frothy cups of milky tea to the gathering who seemed to be relaxing after a hard day's work. Back on the road, Satya could see cabs racing away in the opposite direction ferrying their passengers back to their homes.

'I wish I was in one of those,' she thought wistfully.

It was too late for wishful thinking though. The cab rumbled through the security bars and dropped its load of graveyard shifters at the N.E.W.S. India lobby. Satya's day or night rather, had just begun.

6

THE AMAZING RACE

Holding onto what seemed to be her third coffee that night, Satya slipped off her floaters and curled up in her swivel chair. She leaned forward and increased the volume of the TV next to her computer. She had gotten used to the night shift. It had been a month and a half and counting, but she had stopped complaining. It was not that she had given up on her dreams of reporting or like Shanks decided to switch to production, but she had started to adjust to the situation she was in. And better still, she was trying to make the most of it. The slow pace had helped her hone her technical skills and appreciate the intricacies of production. The edit bays were empty and there was no fighting over voice-over suites. She could afford to give her best to a report because of the low-stress environment. Best of all the company was great.

Aniket was in the night shift with her, along with Keerti Shetty and Sunil Joseph. And Aniket was a blast to hang out with. A towering, heavy built guy, he made it his business to be best friends with every person he came across. He also had the amusing and endearing habit of pretending to flirt with every woman he met. Age no bar and looks the last thing on his mind. And though the flirting was corny and meant absolutely nothing, it still made the 'ladies' smile. Aniket transformed the graveyard shift into happy hours. Satya was glad that she had listened to Rati and gotten over the annoying way in which he had behaved when she was his shadow. These days she looked forward to getting to office to see what Aniket would do or be up to, to brighten up the night shift.

'So what's the most gorgeous woman in the night shift up to? Care for a *cuttings chai* with this humble slave of yours?' the lovable giant called from across the newsroom as he returned to the general desk from an edit bay. As Satya saw him dressed in his trademark bright coloured t-shirt and faded jeans, bearing upon her comfortable workstation, she could not suppress a smile.

'Away with you knave, thou shalt not distract me from my work!' She giggled as she rolled up a newspaper and brandished it at him like a sword.

'And on a more serious note,' she continued, 'I've just finished my third glass of that horrible machine brewed coffee and I don't think I should have any more concoctions for like an hour at least,' she finished with a smile. Aniket held up his hand in a theatrical gesture and brushed off her protests.

'Don't do this to your knave, my fair lady! Ok, ok, that's the most of Shakespearean language I know. Come na yaar. It's 2:30 am and the time when sleep's hitting me the most. I'll get knocked out if I don't get a *chai* energiser right now. And I wouldn't mind a snack either. I don't feel like going alone' he said with the hint of a plea in his voice. Though Satya knew that Aniket was more than capable of going anywhere on his own, she felt herself relenting. After all, she had finished editing a couple of stories and there were no more mails on any further stories. Most of the bulletins had been live the entire day because of the flood situation in some states. She had already edited a few short packages to play in the early morning shows. She knew she could afford to take a break. And what was another tea in the face of the hundreds of cups she had downed in the name of coffee from the disgustingly horrid coffee machine. Satya was sure her stomach had assumed cast-iron proportions thanks to her random eating schedule and the even more random things that she ate. She checked her mail one more time and then made up her mind. There was nothing of any importance in there.

'Ok, fine! But I need to get back in twenty minutes, ok?' she said as she got up and slipped her floaters back on. She brushed some lint off her jeans and ran a cursory hand through her hair. Not like there would be anyone to pass judgement on her hair at half past two in the morning, but it was a habit of hers. Aniket smiled and waited for her to pick up her wallet and join him.

They walked to the elevator lobby through the corridors that were lined with edit suites. The newsroom that bustled with energy during the day was deathly quiet at night. The only sounds were the combined murmurs of the multiple television screens switched on to different channels. Though strictly tuned to news channels during the day shifts, on the nightshift, one could hear drifts of music and well-loved dialogues from re-runs of F.R.I.E.N.D.S, wafting from the screens. Though technically, this was not supposed to be done, it was one of those open secrets that brought the people on the night shift closer to each other.

As Satya and Aniket passed the reporters desk, they saw the sole night reporter deep in conversation with someone who seemed to be his girlfriend on the other end. He was using the office phone and had his head buried in his hands while the receiver was snuggled between his ear and his neck. Though they could not hear him, it was clear from his hunched over pose that he was murmuring sweet nothings to his girlfriend. As they passed him, Aniket bent down and said in a surprisingly female sounding voice, 'Pratyush baby, come have tea *na*. Why are you wasting time talking to her? You said you'd be dumping her *na*?'

With that he moved away swiftly, leaving a furious Pratyush who whipped around, shaking his fist in a threatening manner at Aniket. As Satya and Aniket left the newsroom in peals of muffled laughter, they could hear him desperately explaining to his girlfriend that it was a joke and no, he was honestly not fooling around in the night shift.

It was June and the nights were still warm in NOIDA. The chai vaala had positioned his little box like tea-stall directly in front of the gleaming N.E.W.S India office. As he saw Aniket and Satya approach, a wide smile broke out across his glistening, weary looking face. It had been lean pickings today and this big man always made him smile. Aniket strode across to him and shook his hand gravely, as one would do with a visiting dignitary. Satya who was watching chuckled loudly.

'I'm sure no one else does that to him,' she said.

Aniket smiled at her and turned back to the *chai vaala* and ordered two milky teas and one plate of freshly fried but oily *samosas*. The *chai vaala* sat down to work, pouring out milky tea in two miniscule glasses. Taking the one he pushed towards her from behind his counter, Satya took a sip. It was nothing like the coffee machine slop. This beverage was warm and rich and as she took sips of it, it flowed down her throat giving her a feeling akin to contentment. It also did one more thing. The creamy froth gave her a milk moustache. Aniket made a shaving gesture and pointed at her upper lip. Satya, who was relishing her tea, giggled and wiped it away, only to notice Aniket looking at her.

'What? Why are you staring?' she asked him.

'Just wondering,' he said, 'So what's your scene? I mean, its not like you can see Rehaan. In your words, you are not his type right? Rati told me about what you were speaking of before you got banished to the night shift. And you're too pretty with those big eyes and long hair and killer smile to not be booked already! So what is the scene? Are you seeing someone else? Or are you one of those cold-hearted career women who think it's impossible to care for anything else other than their job?'

Satya laughed at his graphic description.

'First of all, I take offence at you categorising women that way! Women are born multitaskers ok? If you ever doubt that, just ring up your mother for a chat. So Nyaah, to you!' she said sticking her tongue out him.

'But thank you for the compliments. I appreciate them. And as for seeing someone, I'm not… I've been too busy trying to come to terms with this...my work as opposed to what I'd dreamt of myself as. As in lately, it's been all like…let me gather my shattered dreams of making it big on the small screen and adjust to being a cog in the wheel, behind the scenes. I've not had the time or the inclination to see someone or search for someone who can get along with me, in the state that I am at the moment. And also probably 'cos I had a disastrous relationship when I was in college. We ended the relationship exactly a year after we got together. That too, the date was… 9/11! Can you beat that? Never took that as a good omen, so no! Not now, not for a while. What about you?' she threw the query back at him.

Aniket took a long sip of his tea before he replied. He tilted his head as if appraising her.

'Shall I tell you a secret?' he said in a conspiratorial whisper.

'Well, you can tell me your secret in your normal voice you know. There's no one here to eavesdrop unless you're counting the *chai vaala*.' Satya laughed back at his mysterious tone.

'Oho! C'mon *yaar*! I'm serious! Please be serious *na*! So the thing is umm… I don't know how to say this…' Aniket looked embarrassed. He was shuffling his giant feet and wringing the empty paper plate that had held the *samosas.* Satya was looking at him with a bemused expression. Her naturally arched eyebrows were curved upward and her large black eyes had a distinct twinkle. She was having memories of the first time Rehaan had come clean about him being gay.

'Are you ok?' She probed in a tone tinged with mirth.

'Ok, I guess I should just say it at one go. Here goes, I find Rati very attractive and I was wondering if you could help me… I'm just such a big oaf and I don't know… What do you think? Is it too out of this world to work?' he lamely finished looking like a small boy, which was endearing and ludicrous at the same time.

'Awww! I had no idea! I don't know about helping and all baba. Why don't you just tell her yourself? She's so sweet and she's sure to understand you…' Satya said gently. She was touched that Aniket had chosen her to open up to.

'That's the thing she's so sweet, and so used to me flirting with everyone that I'm just scared that she'll feel too sorry for me to say 'no' or worse still think I'm joking! Anyway we need to get back, so enough of all the talk.'

Aniket abruptly switched off his little boy look and went back to the persona Satya was familiar with. By the time they returned to the newsroom, Aniket was back to his normal hale and hearty self. And though he had the security guards and elevator boys in splits with his cheesy one-liners, Satya was looking at him in a different light.

Satya returned to her desk to see a single mail in her inbox. As she sat down to check who it was from, she mentally shut out Pratyush and Aniket who had started off on a mock fight in the background. The sender was P. Govind.

'Oh damn! She knows I took a long break! Someone must have called her! Oh god, why doesn't she just sleep?' Satya frantically thought as she clicked on the mail. Nandan, Kedia and Padma were known in the office as insomniacs who ate, breathed and slept N.E.W.S India.

'Her insomnia's going to be the death of me!' Satya worriedly thought, as the mail seemed to be taking longer than usual to load. When it finally did open, it read as simply as Padma would have spoken to Satya.

"Satya, the flood situation in the country is getting worse. There are feeds from at least five states. Look at all of them. Get information from the news wires. I want a graphics laid report, which will play tomorrow from 5am onwards as a headline report. You can take a by-line and therefore sign off as yourself and not as bureau report, which is the usual practice. I will be waiting to see the report.

Padma"

Satya knew what this meant. It was her one chance to get her visibility back. This was a lifeline that had been thrown out to someone who was floundering in the deep waters of being unappreciated. The fact that Padma would be waiting to see the report reverberated in her head. She checked her watch. It was 3:15 am. She had less than two hours to give her best. She could feel the adrenaline rushing.

The rest of the night passed in a flurry of work. Satya transformed into a whirlwind of activity. She pored over feeds from Maharashtra, Gujarat, Bengal, Orissa and Assam. She scanned through Indian and international agencies like PTI, UNI, Reuters, Associated Press and others. Statistics on destruction, the government departments helping out or washing their hands off their duties, brave individuals in the front of nature's fury- Satya's story had it all. She wrote a script making it as human as possible, while using the figures to back it up.

The biggest challenge however was getting the graphics created and placed on the edited story. The graphics room was on the ground floor. And the graphics producers or 'GFX guys' as they were known insisted on a mail, a phone call after the mail, a face-to-face discussion and then an hour after that to produce the graphic plate. In this case, Satya needed an animated map of India, with red dots with moving concentric circles to pin point the nation's flood affected areas. And for some reason, the graphics producers had chosen that very day to be mind numbingly stubborn and obtuse. First they asked Satya to send a map of India. Next she was summoned to pinpoint where the five flood affected states were.

'How can people without a basic geographic knowledge of their own country be employed by a news channel is something I will never understand,' Satya furiously thought as she dealt with graphics while getting her script in place. Though seemingly simple, the graphics were finally ready only at 4:45 am leaving Satya with exactly ten minutes to complete the story and get it ready for telecast. Every show rundown gets locked five minutes before the show. And the 5am rundown producer was waiting for her headline story. Neena Thakur, the staple anchor of the weekday morning bulletins patted Satya on the head as she walked to the studio, all brushed up and glossy for the show.

'Make it fast kid,' she said encouragingly and walked away. Satya nodded distractedly as she did a double check for audio glitches, edit flashes and other technical problems. Satisfied with her handiwork, she told rundown that they could use her story. As they took over, Satya wiped her sweaty palms on her jeans and walked back to the TV near her desk to watch the show.

It was 4:59 am and the N.E.W.S India logo rolled into life, with the live tag blinking at the right hand corner of the screen. Neena was saying 'Hello, good morning and welcome to the show'. She took a minute to read through the morning headlines. And then she said, 'The flood situation continues to worsen across the nation. Floods have already claimed sixteen lives and wreaked mass destruction. Lets move onto this report from Satyabhama Menon for more details.'

Satya saw the rest of the report in a happy daze. Aniket came and stood behind her,

'Good going princess', he whispered and patted her on the back, with true warmth.

Satya wrapped up her shift with a dreamy smile. She had created a headline story. The bulletin had opened with her name. Production was not as bad as she had made it out to be. She could hardly wait for

Padma's reaction. Though she checked her mail several times, for Padma's response, there was nothing from her. Satya headed home and switched on her TV. Her story was still playing as a headline at 12 pm when she finally slept off, after talking to her friends and family who had called after seeing the report. Before she fell asleep, she had a fleeting thought.

'Strange that I needed someone else's tragedy to feel a sense of personal achievement,' she mused. But then all great award-winning journalists had made their reputation by reporting from war zones or riot stricken areas right? With that justification, Satya quelled the sudden unease she felt about being happy and satisfied with her report. She fell asleep with a slight smile.

It was with a light step that Satya jumped into the pick-up cab that night. She literally ran to her workstation as soon as she reached the newsroom. Switching on the monitor with a flourish, she waited for her mails to load. As she scanned through the hundred odd generic mails that had been sent to all the desk editors, her eyes searched for a mail from an address titled P.govind. And suddenly there it was. She clicked on it frantically. It was in Padma's characteristically simple style.

"Satyabhama is to move to the afternoon shift at the end of this week.

Satya – Good job!

Padma"

Satya sat down in relief. It had paid off. She had never thought that two lines could bring her so much happiness. She had never imagined that she would be this happy to get back to the afternoon shift.

7

ROLLERCOASTER

'No more sidelining,' Satya happily thought as she walked with what she considered her triumphant strut into the newsroom. She had rejoined work in the afternoon shift on a Saturday after her weekly offs. Both days of the weekend had been lean news days. And whomsoever she had bumped into video editors, copywriters and such others, had good words for her flood report. Today was a Monday and all the head honchos would be at work. She walked in with a broad grin, waiting for them to shower her with praise. And as luck would have it, Chetan Roy, co-head of the general desk along with Padma was striding directly towards her. Assuming that he wanted to put in a word about how good the report was, Satya paused and pretended to be looking for something in her bag. After all, she did not want it to be obvious that she was not averse to some appreciation. As she had expected, Chetan gestured to her and stopped by her side.

'Hi, Satya! Just the person I wanted to see!' He said, in his impeccable English accent that just had the slightest hint of the Bengali babu in it. Satya smiled at him, waiting for him to continue, hoping that she looked modest.

'So there's a story we want you to do. It's for the 5pm bulletin so you have around two hours to do it,' he went on. Satya assumed that it must be yet another report where they would need someone as trained as her to get it together in the shortest time.

'Must be the flood aftermath or maybe it's a shoot-out of sorts,' she thought.

'Whatever it is, I know I'll be able to handle it.'

She preened mentally and nodded at Chetan.

'Sure, I'll just dump my stuff by my workstation and come to you for the details.' she said in a tone radiating professionalism, or so she thought.

'Oh, I've already mailed it to you. You were the only *Mallu* in the shift, so you were the obvious choice,' he replied with a smile.

'Oh god! A Kerala story! I hope nothing tragic has happened!' Satya thought.

'I'll get right on it,' she said and started walking purposefully to her desk.

'Great! I just hope that you're not squeamish about creepy crawlies!' Chetan called out after her.

'Creepy crawlies?'

Satya paused and turned and repeated in a mystified tone.

Chetan grinned and said, 'Yup! The story is about a village in Kerala being attacked by giant African snails. Disgusting visuals really! Get it done by 4:45 pm at the latest!' he said as he walked away.

Satya was mortified! She, news trainee who made it to the headlines being asked to edit a package on slugs! Slugs! Why would he say that she was just the person for the job then! With a disgusted expression, she sat down at an edit suite to look at the footage. It was definitely not for the faint hearted. That was true. There were giant slimy snails that were crawling down windowsills, leaving greasy tracks in their wake as they moved at their own pace on people's sitting room floors. It was revolting.

'Why me!' Satya repeatedly thought. And then when she reached the part with the sound bites of the villagers, she got her answer. They were all talking in fluent and rapid Malayalam. Satya gritted her teeth and sat down to work. In a couple of hours as she saw her slug package, close the bulletin, she had to smile. Here she thought that she was now at the top of the pack and would be called in to edit special stories, and there, fate had a different plan for her all together.

'But then that's what NEWS is about. No time to get too big for your boots, 'cos as a news trainee you are always a shoe shine boy!' Satya thought to herself. Then with a smile at the thought, she set off to attend to the rest of the stories of the day.

'You look so different these days...different is not the word, the word is more like radiant' Rati remarked. 'It's like you've finally started to like living here, you've started to adjust'

Rati was sitting across Satya on a marble topped round table, in one of the many coffee bistros in NOIDA. They made a sight for tired eyes. Rati in her light pink kurta teamed with jeans and Satya at her relaxed best in a white tee shirt and her favourite pair of jeans. They had met up for a movie and were killing time at the coffee shop, while they waited for Rehaan to join them for dinner. Aniket was in the afternoon shift and had sullenly and reluctantly gone to work after meeting them for brunch earlier in the day. Both Rati and Satya had their weekly offs and were spending the second day of their two-day off together. Satya looked up from the chicken sandwich she was polishing off and took a long swig of her iced frappucino. She gave Rati a blissful smile as the ice cold drink washed down her throat helping her blot out the memories of the July heat that was swirling around outside.

'Well, yeah! This is the first Sunday off I had. I'm glad I had a Sunday-Monday off and not a proper weekend one. Then we wouldn't have had this common Monday off together,' she said as she reached across and squeezed Rati's hand.

'But this Sunday was particularly good. I took an auto to Delhi with all the money I'd saved up in the night shift… what with the no going out and sleeping through meals and all you know' Satya made a face at Rati.

She continued, 'I had traditional home-cooked food at my relative's place. And my god, it was bliss. I mean I have nothing against North

Indian food. I actually like it a lot. But imagine homemade *Idlis* and *Sambar* and stuff. It was delicious. And if that wasn't enough I met up with Rehaan at Chandni Chowk for street kebabs later. He was in the morning shift *na*, so met up over there around six in the evening. The streets were jam-packed and there were delicious smells wafting from everywhere. All kinds of meaty aromas, mingling with the sweet fragrance of *Attar*... The Jama Masjid towering over us, an imposing structure in the twilight. Look at me going on like some Shakespearean heroine! But I really felt like I'd stepped back into the Mughal era. There are these *mullahs* who are sitting around on the steps of the mosque and they look like they stepped out from the times of Shah Jahan and Aurangazeb. And these women wearing *burkhas*, peering at us through the eye-slits... It's a wonderful experience. Oh and I almost forgot to tell you, Rehaan got accosted by a eunuch who was wearing fantastically garish robes. I almost died of laughter. Needless to say Rehaan was horrified and almost died of fright. Ask him about it when he comes ok? Speaking of which, he was supposed to meet up with us around 6 pm na. Where is the guy? It's almost 6:30 and he's not called or messaged either. Hmmm, anyway he should be calling in soon.'

Satya checked her phone to see if there was any message from Rehaan. She kept the phone on the table after seeing nothing from him or anyone else.

'Ya, don't worry. He must be caught up at work or something. Anyway Chandni Chowk sounds amazing. I've only gone till Daryganj for the Sunday book market. And then shopping of course! Never in the sweetmeats area! Call me next time you guys plan to go,' Rati pleasantly said.

Satya smiled and looked at Rati who was having a chocolate pastry along with an iced cappuccino. Though Rati tended to be slightly plumper than was usual in the diet-obsessed broadcast world, she was the only person Satya had never heard complaining about her weight. She always had her warm smile on and a flawless complexion that made most in the newsroom envious. No one had ever heard her crib about her job as well. Rati smiled with obvious glee about her pastry and gave Satya a wide grin, with her front teeth partially covered with chocolate. It made her look as if half of her teeth had rotted away. Satya did a double take and giggled.

'You look like a two-year old with chocolate smattered all over her face' she laughed and continued, 'And of course. Next time I'll call you in advance. So how was your weekend? What were you up to?'

'Well, I spent three hours in a parlour, got a massage, got a pedicure, came out feeling absolutely gorgeous. Then I picked up a couple of movie DVDs from sector 18 and went home. I ended up cooking dinner, watching the movies and generally relaxing. A perfect Sunday actually.'

Rati ended her recital with a smile. She did look happy enough with her single existence.

'But it would not harm anyone to do a little bit of match making would it?' Satya thought, and the best way forward for that was always 'the shock and awe' policy.

'Oh I thought you would have hung out with Aniket?' she casually threw in. Rati looked surprised at the thought.

'Huh? Really? We usually see each other only at work. Why would you think that?' she said.

Satya recklessly ploughed on.

'Well, it's just that you guys look so sweet…' She trailed off mid-sentence as her phone started to ring.

'Oho, wait a sec! That must be Rehaan with some lame excuse about being late!' she said as she picked up the phone, leaving a perplexed looking Rati across the table.

'Oh great! He's calling from one of the office phones! Mr.- I-want -to -be -known -as -the best –TV- reporter must be doing after hours.' Satya caustically remarked.

'Hello Rehaan *saahab*! Why are you so … Oh! Hello!' Satya abruptly stopped talking and moved her head from side to side, as she looked at Rati. It was not Rehaan on the other end of the line.

'Satya, there has been a blast in the local trains in Mumbai. At this moment, we are getting information that there are multiple blast sites. All desk editors are being called back. You need to get in to office as soon as possible. Please pass on the message to others who you think are on leave but live in the vicinity. Please come in as soon as possible.' Padma's clear and measured tones rang out in Satya's ears.

'I am in NOIDA, Padma. Rati is with me. We will come in right away. And I will pass on the message.' Satya replied calmly. But as she hung up, her hands were shaking. Rati looked alarmed at Satya's suddenly pale face.

'What happened? Why did Padma call?' she urgently asked.

'Mumbai... blasts on the local trains', Satya said in a wobbly voice as she scrolled down her contacts list on her phone trying to call her friends in Mumbai. Rati got up and tugged at Satya's hand.

'We need to get to office. We'll make our calls on the way.' She threw down some money on the table to cover the bill and pulled Satya out of the bistro.

It seemed to Satya, that every call she had made, had taken an eternity to connect. Every un-answered call had left her with a feeling of an unspeakable dread. Yet by the time, she reached the N.E.W.S India office, she had managed to contact most of her friends and family in the city. Satya's friends assured her that they would contact everyone she had not been able to get in touch with and call back as soon as they could.

Rati and Satya ran towards Padma who was supervising the breaking news flashes. Tina was at the ticker desk. Padma turned towards them with an uncharacteristically grim face.

'Do you have friends and family in Mumbai? Are they ok?' she gravely asked. Satya gave her a barely perceptible nod as Rati said that her friends were safe.

'We have lots of work girls,' Padma said switching the subject grimly.

'Rati, I want you to take over the ticker for a while, so that Tina can catch her breath. I will assign you to something else after that,' she then turned to Satya and said, 'Our entire Mumbai Bureau is fanned out across the city with their outdoor broadcast vans. Footage is coming in from various sites. I want you to monitor this. Get an edit bay for yourself. I need the visuals in the headlines updated, every time anything new comes in. Whenever we have a live phone-in with a reporter, you need to get the visuals for that ready. Remember that you can show blood and injured victims. Edit out the dead bodies as much as you can. And no blurred shots or shots where the camera movements are too jerky. Am I clear? Now off you go! I'll let you know what you have to do next later.' Without waiting for Satya's answer, Padma walked off to her desk, where her fellow desk heads were waiting for her. Satya dumped her bag at her workstation and became one amongst the jostling many in the newsroom.

Nandan was there, right in the middle of the newsroom. He was on the phone, barking out instructions to the many reporting units that were on duty in Mumbai. News was pouring in about the blasts from other parts of the city as well. Nandan was explaining to the younger ones amongst the reporters to stay calm as they did live news reports and to not even mention the whiff of a rumour before it had been confirmed. Misreporting at a time like this could spell certain doom for the channel. Nandan constantly proved why he could own an operation this size. He took editorial decisions, whipped into the studio, did live shows on the actual situation and called up government officials on-air for some hard-hitting questions.

In complete contrast to him however, the complete unpredictability of the situation seemed to have transformed Kedia into a blithering idiot. He was 'Eh-ing' his way through the chaos of it all. Nandan had told him to take complete responsibility for the input desk. Every news channel has a limited amount of incoming frequencies on which footage can be beamed in to the headquarters. It is the input desk, which takes a call on which reporter's footage gets uploaded first, if there are two or more reports in queue. This usually depends on which story is more newsworthy. But in a situation like this, someone senior has to take a call. It's impossible to decide whether the story of the family killed on their way to an outing is more newsworthy and tragic than the report on the young entrepreneur who was killed on his way back after his first day in office. Kedia was proving himself to be totally incapable of holding his own. It seemed like Kedia had a position of power only because he had stuck on to the same job unwaveringly and then managed to befriend Nandan. It was almost like he was making it clear why no one had ever heard of him before. Anyone watching the way he was handling the situation could make out, that he had no calibre whatsoever. He was rushing to Nandan every five minutes when multiple streams of footage from Mumbai, clogged the queue. Most of the input editors looked ready to burst from the high-pressure situation they were working in. Some of them looked like they wanted to murder Kedia. But when you are behind the scenes, speaking up in protest is akin to professional hara-kiri. And so the input desk soldiered on with their incompetent leader.

The flow of information was immense. There were visuals of the burnt bogies, the great number of dead and dying, the clammed-up government officials, hard working security and rescue forces and the most tragic of them all- the people who had arrived at the scene in search of their loved ones. Satya could not afford to let her emotions take over. Her channel needed her. And the thousands of viewers watching them needed these visuals, so that the tragedy that had happened in Mumbai could be shown to them, almost at the speed of real time. As the hours passed, the footage became increasingly from the hospitals, where the injured had been taken. And then the human vultures started moving in to the city, to spout their killing clichés. Reporters started sending in sound bites from politicians and page three celebrities who were ensconced in their air conditioned offices and cars, lamenting about how the spirit of Mumbai had received yet another tragic blow.

Satya had now been put to the task of editing these sound bites. As she went through platitude after platitude, Satya found only a handful, who were ready to actually roll up their sleeves and help in whichever way they could. As she hurriedly readied each clip for telecast, Satya thought, in a corner of her mind, 'But how can we blame these losers for being fake and mouthing all their insincere garbage? It's us the media who's giving them a platform to speak in the first place! If we didn't bother telecasting their bites and publishing their quotes, they wouldn't be who they are today! But if we didn't have them, what would we use to fill the space in between the gory visuals?'

It was an unpleasant thought and Satya did not want to dwell on it. Not now anyway. She immersed herself in her work.

The chaos gradually slowed down to the normal order of business. By 11:30 pm, the newsroom was almost back to its usual pace. Yet one could still see the occasional panic- stricken person. People continued to run from the feed room to the edit bay. And one could hear the snippets of the loud, high-octane conversation Nandan was having, with yet another reporter out on the field. Satya was rechecking one of the bites to be telecast, when one of the general desk heads, Aneesh Ramnath called out to her. Perpetually dressed in tight fitting t-shirts and jeans, at the age of forty-five, Aneesh looked like he was desperately missing his long gone twenties. Satya completed her edit and walked over to Aneesh.

'Satya, good job! Now I need you to make this really emotional news report on the blasts. The Mumbai reporters are still stationed at various sites. So we will need this report to be structured from here. I've put Rati on the information angle story. Your angle is tears, tears and more tears.'

Aneesh's tone struck Satya as a little callous. Mentally shrugging it off as a possible way of suppressing his stress, Satya nodded for him to continue.

Aneesh went on, 'So start with the story of the girl who found her brother's body at the hospital and pile on information, from all the other high emotion stories there. I want tears running down viewer's cheeks. I don't want a single dry eye. You get the brief, right? Now take your time, 'cos it's only midnight and we need this only for the 5 am bulletin. Right then!' And with that Aneesh walked off.

Satya was more than disconcerted by his attitude. By then she was exhausted by the constant exertion, and decided to catch a quick snack before sitting down to work again. People had been pulled from all other desks like the international, business and sports desks. And as a result, Satya found herself at the office canteen dinner along with Rehaan, Shanks, Rati and Aniket. Tina was sitting with Keerti and Debashree at a neighbouring table. It seemed to be an unspoken agreement that everyone was staying back, for as long as they could. The shifts did not matter today. Dinners at the canteen were usually light affairs with a lot of banter and teasing. Today there was an air of fatigue, and the only noise was that of the spoons clattering on the plates and the steel glasses clinking against each other. Everyone had friends and family in Mumbai. No one was in the mood for any small talk.

Rati had done five straight hours of breaking news flashes and had blood-shot eyes. She put her head down on the table with a deep sigh. Without uttering a single word or a wisecrack, as was characteristic of him, Aniket got up and got a plate of Parathas for her. He had also kept a small chocolate éclair on the plate. He placed the plate on the table and tenderly patted her shoulder. Rati lifted her head and slowly took the plate. Her eyes misted over, she reached out and took Aniket's hands. In the face of the tragedy they had just seen, Rati's simple act of reaching out for Aniket, seemed to Satya like a re-affirmation in all those things that she thought were scarred, and lost by the depraved acts of a few. As they all continued to have their dinner, Rati and Aniket were holding hands and picking at their food in silence, but with slight smiles.

All of Satya's friends had called in from Mumbai, fortunately safe and sound. Rehaan had been in office since seven in the morning, when he had come in for his shift. He was on the verge of collapse and now heading home. Satya had just gotten back to work, after seeing him to an office cab. She had the report to produce. The footage was traumatic. Cameras from various channels were trawling the hospitals for human-interest stories and high-powered emotions. And they had found their hapless story. A young woman they had focused on had just found her brother's body. He had been returning home after college. She had burst into hysterical tears, in full view of the media. N.E.W.S India's persistent reporters had managed to get a few unintelligible words from her, as they had shoved the microphone in her face. There were visuals of her calling her parents and slumping down on the hospital floor. Swallowing a lump in her throat and brushing away the tears that welled up in her eyes, Satya set about editing the report.

Around three am, she put her headphones down and tried to give herself a neck massage. She could feel massive stress knots at the nape of her neck. She decided to get Aneesh to check her report, before she could leave for the day. Satya could feel waves of exhaustion wash over her. She headed towards Aneesh's desk and told him that the story was ready. He walked back to the edit bay with her, to take a look at the report. As Aneesh put on the headphones over his head for a listen, Satya rubbed her palms over her tired eyes. A minute and a half later, he slipped the headphones off and gave Satya a half frown.

'Well it's definitely good. But there is no… what do you say…

zing to it… No *Masala*! Throw in music, a couple of close-ups, make that a lot of close-ups and then we're done.'

Satya looked at him, as if she could not believe what he had just said.

'What?' she managed to reply.

'You know, *Masala*! Like spice it up!' he casually replied as he started to walk away.

'But Aneesh, her story is tragic enough. Do we really need special effects? The viewers are going to feel her pain anyway, right?' Satya replied emotionally.

Aneesh half turned and said 'Listen, I know it's been a long day Satya, but you need to get on with it. We see so many tragic stories in a day, double the number in a week. Children killed, families mowed down in freak accidents, riots, fires … you name it! How many stories do you recall? Add the music and the effects and you can expect some recall that's all,' he shrugged and walked off.

With a mutinous expression, Satya got back to work. She was sure that Padma would take one look and demand the simpler version to go on air. But she would put in the effects anyway, so that Aneesh would see how wrong he was. She slaved on it for another hour. It was 4 am when she finally finished working on it. She had ended up ignoring every tenet of journalism that she had learnt, right from "Never use close-ups when the subject is in grief. It denotes the intrusion of privacy" to the cardinal rule of "Keep it simple. Let the story narrate itself".

She trudged to the news editors' desk and sulkily told Aneesh that she had made the required changes. This time around, Padma too came along with Aneesh, to see the completed story. Satya waited for both of them to finish watching the stories individually. She waited for vindication as Padma slipped off the headphones.

'Here it comes,' she thought, 'Padma's going to blast Aneesh for having the sensibilities of a tacky B-grade Bollywood director.'

Padma looked at Satya and simply said, ' Very good Satya. Good work today. Inform rundown that they can use this story. Go home and come in a little later for your shift today afternoon.

'Well done Satya! You really got the brief,'Aneesh added.

Satya was speechless. She could feel tears welling up. The day had been long and cruel. She felt like she had learnt some unpleasant lessons, which she wished she could ignore. She managed to say a brisk goodnight and walked away. Grabbing her stuff, she called for an office cab and headed for home.

Though Satya was drained of all energy and the will to stay awake, the images she had seen today were flitting in front of her eyes, keeping her from sleeping. After what seemed like hours of seeing the same images in a loop, she slipped off into a fitful, restless sleep.

The next day Satya found herself unable to relax as the aftermath of the blasts were looming like dark clouds over her. Ignoring Padma's offer to report in later than usual, Satya went to work on time. Most of the bosses were on leave after the previous day's all-nighter. They seemed to be working from home though. Satya's inbox was filled with congratulatory mails from most of the heads of department including Nandan, Padma and even a grudging one from Debashree. They all appreciated her special treatment of the story, apart from the hard work, she had put in. But Satya could not find it in her to muster the same happiness she had felt at being praised for her story on the floods. She felt like there was something very wrong, with no one finding a problem with the fact that tragedy had to be jazzed up for viewers to feel and understand it.

As she continued to read through her mails, something caught her eye. It was a mail from Kedia, '*Good job Satya! Been watching your work! Come meet me, next Monday, 11:30 am!*

Ram Kedia'

As she shut her mailbox to move on to the stories of the day, Satya reflected on Kedia's mail,

'Now what was that all about!

8

PROJECT WEATHERVANE

11:15am, a bright and sunny Monday in July, and Satya was waiting outside Kedia's office. She was still in the afternoon shift and had to report to her desk only by 3 pm. So she was hoping that the meeting would be short, and that she could head for a leisurely lunch before starting on work. Yesterday had been a gruelling day.

One of the senior producers, Avantika Suri had wanted a report on war ships using Indian ports for refuelling. Satya had attempted to look busy but Avantika's keen eyes had seemed to see through her mock busy pose. As she called out to her, the rest of the team at the desk editor's desk had made sympathetic groans. No one liked working for Avantika. A self-proclaimed producer extraordinaire trained in the United Kingdom, Avantika was the newsroom's resident diva. With extremely short hair that was spiked up to resemble a punk rocker, Avantika was also stick thin. She had a pale face and as if to highlight the paleness, she used a navy blue eye shadow and some heavy Kajal on her eyes. A vociferous supporter of PETA, she would wear faux fur coats in the middle of summer to the newsroom.

'This is to make a point!' she would declare in her British accented voice as she strutted around on heels.

'The only point she's making is that, not all's right in her head!' Rehaan had muttered to Satya once. Satya tended to agree with him. Avantika was also prone to tantrums that would put film stars to shame. It was with quite a lot of trepidation that Satya started off on the report. It seemed straightforward enough. Avantika had called for footage from all the coastal bureaus for interesting shots. She had asked the Feed room to record them under a specific name, and with a numerical tag, so that Satya could access them easily from the hundreds of feed that came in on a daily basis. However when Satya sat down to sift through the feed, it seemed like Avantika's directions had been far from clear. She found 'KOL_POLCE_1' for the corrupt Kolkata police story, 'MUM_BlST_FLLW' for the Mumbai blasts follow up report and 'GOA- GO_TRSM' for a Goa tourism and so on and so forth. But there was nothing to indicate any footage on war ships of any sort. She searched again and again.

The feed room folk were notorious for their typos. They put down feed names as the feed came in while they had one ear glued to a phone, talking to the bureau that was sending it. As the feed came in they would take down the story name as they heard it and simultaneously listened to the feed for any audio glitches as well as checked it for any video glitches. It was a tough job all right and everyone agreed. But they still wished that the feed room would listen to the name of the report a little harder. More often than not, they put down 'Babies story' instead of 'Rabies story' or gibberish like 'Our age story' for 'Garbage story' making the desk editor or the news trainee's job just a little harder.

Satya found herself cursing the feed room yet again as she waded through the feed. She had tried every kind of search term. 'War' and the response was 'Sorry, no feed with that term', 'Ships', same response, 'Refuel', same response. Satya was getting frustrated. She had spent half an hour on what should have ideally taken ten minutes. Avantika had given her three hours and for Avantika that meant two and a half hours and the rest spent in nagging. Satya hurried across to Avantika's desk.

'Umm... Avantika, what did you ask the feed room to name the footage?' she asked hesitantly. Avantika turned with an expression worthy of the greatest hams of all actors.

'What? My dear child, you still have not found the footage? This is a tragedy! Warships, child, warships! Come with me!'

She gathered the hem of the long, flouncy black skirt she was wearing and glided away in the direction of the feed room search station. Satya rolled her eyes discreetly and followed. Avantika was bent over the keyboard and pressing on the enter key with force. The search terms 'Warships' or 'War' or 'Ships' were returning no results. Avantika's face contorted with mild fury. She was prone to exaggerated mood swings anyway. Satya inadvertently took a step back. Avantika swished her skirt and strode to the feed room looking like an impoverished queen on the warpath.

Satya hung back. She sometimes had coffee with the feed room folks. Witnessing their embarrassment at the hands of Avantika would put an end to that. She heard apologetic noises and exasperated ones. And finally an annoyed high-pitched 'Goodness gracious' from Avantika. She came out looking supremely irritated. Behind her a red faced Suresh framed the feed room doorway, wringing his hands, looking like he hoped his ordeal was over. Avantika bent over the keyboard again and furiously jabbed at the keys. Looking over her shoulder, Satya saw that the search had returned four streams of footage.

'Get to work child. Two hours more,' she said ominously and walked away. Satya nodded and sat down to run through the visuals. But before that she wanted to know what exactly had the feed name been. She took a look, did a double take and burst out laughing. Catching Avantika glaring at her, she quickly swallowed her mirth and ran in search of an edit suite. Later that evening, as she waited for her office cab, she ran into a dejected Suresh who said, '*Woh na*… I don't know *yaar*! She came in and said it with an accent, and you know the kind of rush we have in the feed room. She kept moving her hands and *phir* moving her head. *Toh*, I just typed what I heard. 'Whoreships' I typed in panic. I thought it was some prostitution smuggling scandal! You never know *na*?'

Satya burst out laughing the second time that day. She told him to cheer up as Avantika rarely held a grudge and headed to her cab.

'My office is like a circus. You never know what the next act is going to bring!' she thought with a smile.

'Oho, which reminds me! Tomorrow I need to meet Mr Eh! God

knows what that is all about!'

Kedia was not in his cabin, but then Satya had turned up earlier than required. She waited patiently, smiling to herself remembering the 'Whoreship' episode. As she stood, one foot crossed backwards, leaning on the wall and hands in her pockets, she saw a slew of familiar faces approaching.

'Must be off to the coffee machine,' she thought. But then she figured that, that could not be the answer as some amongst the group were on the night shift, and it was highly unlikely that they were still here. Usually people on the night shift were on the verge of falling asleep almost as soon as they got inside the cars, which dropped them back in the morning. There was no reason for them to stay back unless there had been a breaking news situation and they had been asked to pitch in. Satya had checked the bulletin before she had headed towards Kedia's office. It was an average news day, and there were enough people on the shift to take care of the corresponding news flow. So then why was this bunch still here?

'Hey guys! What's up?' she called out. They seemed extremely relieved to see her. The group comprised of Keerti Shetty, Sunil Joseph, Lini Advaith, Vaidehi Lal and Vidya Saran. While Satya was friends with Sunil and Vidya, she had just a 'Hi-Bye' sort of relationship with the rest.

Keerti was a petite girl with the silkiest hair possible. Unfortunately, her hair seemed to dominate her personality and by default, her conversations. She was someone who would never need anyone else to handle her publicity. She managed to do that single-handedly. Self-promotion in her mind meant big time promotion in real life. That's exactly what she did. Needless to say, Satya who hated talking about herself or her achievements and least of all her appearance, had nothing in common with Keerti. They had barely exchanged any words even though they had been on the same shift several times. Keerti's ultimate goal was to make it big in the fashion world. She had joined a channel in the hopes of going on-air somehow, in whatever capacity possible, so that some model scout somewhere would see her and she would eventually become a model. She was too short to opt for the tried and tested methods of participating in a beauty pageant.

Lini Advaith however, had no such issues. She made heads turn each time she walked into the newsroom. Tall, dark and stunning, Lini was no bird brain either. However she had no problems in using her charms to get a promotion, if her intelligence did not seem to make the required impact. Satya had met up with her for coffee, a couple of times and enjoyed the conversation. It had been light and breezy peppered with Bollywood gossip, and if that was not enough, there was always office gossip as a fall back topic. Yet even while laughing with her about the office grapevine, Satya found herself thinking about how Lini always casually omitted mentioning certain things. Things like how her dinner date with one of the senior anchors, had been just a day before she had gotten a chance to try her hand at reporting. And this had not been a one-off case. All the opportunities Lini had gotten at work were linked with a social engagement she had, had with someone senior the previous day. No one ever spoke about it openly, but it was whispered about in the office most of the time. Satya had somehow found it hard to not judge Lini's easy work ethics.

Vaidehi Lal however, did not seem to have a problem with it. She and Lini were always together. It seemed as if the desk heads had also recognised that they worked better when put on the same shift and put them together. Known as the 'Twins' to their face, 'Vaidehi' and Lini were called the 'Siams' behind their back. However, Vaidehi was not as gorgeous as her twin. A slightly horsy jaw marred what would otherwise have been a classically beautiful face. She was good at her work though and pleasant to hang around with.

But given a choice, Satya knew that she would prefer to spend time with Sunil and Vidya. Much like herself and Rehaan, they had been the best of friends from college and were definitely not a couple. Vidya had a long-time boyfriend back in her hometown Lucknow, and Sunil was rumoured to have a not so secret crush on Lini. However, she had never shown the slightest bit of interest in him, while she continued to be polite in their office encounters. Sunil however never held it against her, as he thought her to be way above his league anyway. Sunil considered himself thin, gawky and in the possession of a very average face.

'No way, am I going to get the courage to speak to her!' he used to say disparagingly. Satya thought that he was short-selling himself and completely ignoring his show-stopping smile. Vidya, on the other hand knew that she was pretty, with her brown eyes, which crinkled each time she smiled and the cutest button nose. Though her looks did not dominate her personality, she was hard working and one of those rare desk editors who actually liked what she did. Satya had enjoyed working with her whenever they had been on the same shift.

As the group came to a halt by Kedia's door, it was Sunil who spoke up.

'Thank God, you're here too! We're just discussing Kedia's mail man…'

Keerti cut in, 'We thought we were being pulled up or fired or something! But we saw you in the distance and were just saying that if Satya's here, it's probably not a 'buck-up' lecture! You're one of their favourites! The phoenix that rose from the night shift', she finished.

'That seemed to be a tad snide!' Satya thought. But she chose to ignore it, and spoke to Vidya instead.

'So all of you got the mail? The Monday meeting one?'

Vidya nodded and replied, 'Yep! And none of us have a clue'

'But we'll know soon enough! It's 11:25, he should be getting here any minute,' Lini trilled. No sooner had she said that, the group heard Kedia's voice.

'All you lovely ladies and gentlemen here early, eh? Hmmmm. There are too many of you to fit into my office. Head towards the conference room and give me two minutes, eh? I will be right there with you.' With that, Kedia walked into his cabin. He had seemed uncharacteristically cheerful.

'That must be the nearest to his pleasant tone!' Satya thought, as the group traipsed to the conference room.

Two minutes later they were seated and whispering about the many possible reasons that they had been called in there. Keerti, Lini and Vaidehi were bunched together on one side, while Satya was sitting with Sunil and Vidya. The one thing that they all agreed on, was that Kedia seemed much nicer than he had ever seemed before. Putting an end to the discussion, Kedia walked in and gave a smile of sorts. He positioned himself at the head of the table and continued to stand. While the group started to get up, he motioned them to remain seated and started off.

'OK! So we've been observing all of you eh! We have an opportunity for you. It's quite a rare one. But the catch is, that there are six of you here, and only two openings.'

At this point he gravely looked around at the room, surveying each and every one of them, with the expression of a general sending his troops to war. It was surreal.

'My God! Am I in some kind of a bizarre nightmare where I'm one of the participants in a reality show? Sure seems like one!'

Satya pinched herself to make sure she was not asleep. The angry red welt that sprang up on her arm was proof that she was certainly not asleep and in fact quite wide-awake. Kedia seemed to notice her squirming and directed the rest of his remarks mostly at her.

'You all know Menaka Sinha, eh?'

They all nodded vigorously, especially Sunil who had a not so secret crush on the very sexy weather woman too, like half the male population in the newsroom did. Menaka was the anchor of the weather bulletin for the nine 'o' clock news through the week. She was in her early thirties, rumoured to be a former Miss India finalist, and Nandan's ex in the distant past, said to have acted in a couple of Bollywood movies as the heroine's friend and always looked like she had stepped out of the pages of a fashion magazine. She also behaved, as if she was doing everyone a favour by deigning to read the weather report for a channel like N.E.W.S India. But then she did make sure that everyone noticed her.

Looking suitably pleased at the group's reaction, Kedia continued, 'So Menaka's moving into the entertainment desk as an anchor, eh. And our morning weather person Amit is leaving us to head for higher studies abroad. So we decided to pick those of you guys who were doing well, and give you this opportunity to ... how do you say it ... fight it out eh?'

He looked around with wolfish eagerness to see how his statement had gone down with the group. This time the reaction was mixed. The Siams and Keerti let out whoops of excitement. Sunil looked thoughtful and his pose said it all. He was sitting with his chin balanced delicately on the back of his palm. Vidya and Satya found themselves looking at each other at the same time, with expressions that were mirror images. They had both raised an eyebrow each and were looking at each other with quizzical expressions. Kedia grinned showing his yellowed teeth, which Satya supposed was a beam as far as his smile went.

He continued, 'Menaka has agreed to audition you, eh! This is in two weeks. She leaves for the entertainment desk in Mumbai, in a month. So after the auditions, the chosen ones will have intensive training for two weeks. And then you're on-air eh? Excited?'

Kedia looked around at the group. He was probably looking for slavish expressions of gratitude, at the opportunity that he had just bestowed upon them. While three of the group had expressions that were quite close, Satya, Sunil and Vidya were projecting otherwise. Satya and Vidya were still looking at each other.

Satya could sense that Vidya was thinking the same thing as her, which was more or less, 'What sort of training does a weather girl need?' Cutting straight across their thoughts, Kedia abruptly called the meeting to a halt.

'All right then! So Menaka will mail you on the exact date and timing. Start preparing, eh! Now get back to work, those of you who are in the morning shift. The rest can start preparing, eh! Best of Luck! I will be waiting to see who wins the challenge. Ok, I have work.'

With that dismissive remark Kedia turned and walked out. Keerti, Lini and Vaidehi were furiously whispering amongst themselves and walked out at great speed as if to avoid any discussion with the rest. Vidya and Satya were about to launch into a discussion of their own, when Sunil piped up.

'Guys, we have to do this later! We're on the morning shift and Padma will be keeping an eye out for us. Satya are you free later?'

'No, I'm in the afternoon shift. But I'm off tomorrow, so we can meet up in Sector eighteen. For brunch? Is that cool?' Satya asked.

'Great, we'll see you tomorrow then. I'll text you,' Vidya replied for both of them. She gave Satya a quick hug and followed Sunil out of the room.

'Hmmm, it's a bright and sunny day with scattered showers,' Satya murmured to herself as she walked away.

'Weather girl? Weather girl? You?'

Rehaan somehow managed to blend a dash of scorn and a generous dollop of bewilderment seamlessly, in his surprised exclamation.

'Pipe down Rehaan!' an embarrassed Satya said, looking around and making apologetic faces at the diners around them. They were having coffee and sandwiches at a bistro inside the Centre Stage mall in NOIDA. Satya had met up with Sunil and Vidya earlier in the day. They had left unsure of whether this was a good opportunity at all. Sunil was the only one who was excited about it, while Satya and Vidya were still trying to analyse the reasons behind them being short-listed. Satya had decided to break the news to Rehaan, in the evening. And this was how he had reacted, by shrieking like a soon to be headless chicken. Rehaan lowered his volume at her furious and frantic gestures.

'But how come you were selected for the group to audition? That's so funny!'

Rehaan went on in a slightly calmer tone. Satya did not know whether to feel complimented or insulted.

'Do you think I'm not pretty enough to be in the group?' she asked in a small voice.

'No, that's the thing Tya! That's precisely the thing! Reading the weather is not reporting! A weather woman is not a journalist unless she's out in the front, reporting the Tsunami. Or if she works for an international channel, where you need to know about wind currents and sea currents. Some of them have even studied metrology. In our country, we've not evolved to that stage yet! I think it's your looks that have landed you this audition, because I don't think the post requires any other specialisation in Indian news channels. And you've always wanted people to go beyond your looks. This is not what you want, right?' he asked forcefully. Satya obviously agreed with him.

'I know Rehaan! This is exactly what Vidya and I were discussing. And I was talking to Mum about the same. But even though she wasn't excited, she said it was an opportunity and that if I turn it down, the channel's going to think that I don't jump at opportunities. Where does that leave me?' Satya said reflectively while stirring her coffee slowly.

'Hmmm...I get it. It does look bad if you turn it down. That's true. But I don't want you stuck as a weather woman! You're way too smart for that Tya!'

Rehaan thumped his fist on the table emphatically, making a few drops of coffee jump out of Satya's mug. This time, Satya did not bother to calm him. She felt as confused as Rehaan looked annoyed at the turn of events.

As the designated two weeks of preparation time started to slip by her, Satya found herself watching more and more weather bulletins and flipping through the weather forecasts in newspapers. Though she tried to think of mock bulletins in her head, she could not bring herself to muster the same excitement she saw in the 'Siams' and Keerti. They had adopted a formal style of dressing and had started wearing shirts and jackets despite it still being July. To Satya, it seemed like they had already picked out their wardrobes to project themselves as N.E.W.S India's next top weatherwomen. Sunil seemed to be enjoying the idea too these days, however Vidya remained non-committal. Despite long debates and discussions with her parents and Rehaan, Satya had figured that she was still on the fence with this one. She decided to go with the flow. She also decided to wear a semi-formal black shirt with jeans for the audition. After all, when faced by Keerti and the Siams, she did not want it to seem that she had not made even the slightest of efforts.

And the day finally dawned. Much like the perfect weather forecast, it was all clear skies with no clouds anywhere. The group assembled at Studio Three, where the auditions were slated to start at 10 am sharp. And on the dot she appeared. Menaka Sinha looked much like a Barbie doll, every strand of hair blow dried and straightened and every bit of visible skin powdered and bronzed. The only two in the group who did not like either her looks, or her vibes were predictably Satya and Vidya. Menaka seemed a bit too plastic for their taste and a tad too patronising, as she belted out directions and instructions. Not to mention the dumbing down, she was subjecting them to.

'You can see that there is a green screen behind me, as I talk about the weather. On some occasions, it is blue. But it is never the map, which you see on screen. This is known as the chroma key process. The weather map, which you see on air, is of course, projected on to this background. So weather reading is a highly complex manoeuvre. You stand up with your back to a blank, yet coloured background. You look at the script, which comes on the auto-cue, or your tele prompter and you read it and smile slightly while you do this. But you must remember not to smile when you are forecasting torrential rains or drought! That is not nice!'

'Really? Who would have thought of that?' Satya thought sarcastically. Menaka sounded like a crystal gazer passing on her forecasting talents, as she spoke in a slightly husky tone. The Siams seemed to be taking copious notes. Satya noticed this, caught Vidya's eye and rolled her eyes at her. Menaka must have seen the gesture as she paused and cleared her throat, before continuing with her patronising monologue.

'Weather reporting is a great talent. It's not just about the script. Did you know that you point to the back with your right hand, when you're talking about the North and Central India? And when we talk about the east and the south, you have to step forward, move sideways, switch arms and then point. All of this while we continue to smile. I know this sounds complicated, but its possible.' Menaka said with pompous earnestness.

This time Satya could not stop herself from chuckling out loud. It was clear Menaka noticed this time. She threw Satya a furious look, at which Satya hastily transformed the laugh into a hacking cough.

Menaka went on, 'Some of you think this is easy. They will have to go through the process, for a change in perceptions. We will have one rehearsal and the second attempt will be taped. You will come in individually. We will give you the results tomorrow. We will go alphabetically. So that means the order will be Keerti, Lini, Satyabhama, Sunil, Vaidehi and Vidya.'

The auditions had begun. Keerti walked in and the rest milled around the studio entrance, with cups of coffee. While all of them looked nonchalant, you could make out that the group was nervous, by the slight shaking of one's hand or the high-pitched laughter of another. Keerti came out happy and excited, trilling about the positive feedback she got on her stellar performance. As Lini went in, Satya could feel her heart beating a little bit faster. While she did not see herself as the next top weatherwoman, she did not want to be the worst performer either. It would be awful to be bad at something, which you had mocked and made fun of. Then she would be more like the fox with his sour grapes, than the smart reporter who considered herself to be above weather reporting. As she tossed the thoughts around in her mind, Lini walked out beaming. Suddenly, it was Satya's turn.

It was freezing in the studio and Satya felt her hands go numb. This was not entirely due to the sub-zero temperatures in the studio. Her nerves were also contributing to the situation. And Menaka's icy glare was not helping either.

'Oh! So, here we are! It's the comic's turn. Why does Kedia think that comedians would make good weatherwomen? I don't know. But still sent in by the big bosses… So go on, lets see what you can do.'

Satya did not bother to retort and positioned herself in front of the background.

'Well, start off then!' Menaka half-snarled.

'Good morning and welcome to the weather report,' Satya began.

'No, that's not a proper tone. Be chirpier! Repeat from the beginning.'

Menaka cut in, in a tone that seemed to border on indifference. Satya had no option, but to start again. She infused a tone of mock cheer and started again.

'Welcome to the weather bulletin, we...'

'No, no! You always take a toss from the anchors. You never start with a welcome,' Menaka interrupted again. It did not take long for Satya to figure what Menaka was playing at. She was just venting her irritation for Satya's flippancy in the morning. Satya figured that this was one situation she could not get out of. An apology would prove that she had not taken the morning instructions seriously. And losing her temper would only worsen the situation. She decided to be stoic about it. After all there was no way out of it.

By the end of it all however, Satya felt like Menaka had elevated nitpicking and criticism, to an art form. From Satya's accent, to the way her arm bent, to a non-existent crease in her shirt, to the importance of wearing make up and having poker-straight hair, Menaka picked on each and every one of Satya's real or perceived flaws. By the time they were ready to tape the audition, Satya was drained. And though she managed to read through the script in one take, the footage had a fatigued quality to it. Satya felt that if there was a level lower than rock bottom then she had just hit it. Satya did not bother to thank Menaka as she walked out, pushing the studio doors harder than necessary.

When the results were mailed to them the next day, it was Vaidehi who was the most surprised of the lot. Keerti and Lini were the chosen ones. And in what seemed like a fit of some extra spite, Menaka had mailed the names of the hopefuls, along with those who had been selected, to the entire office. Now the entire newsroom seemed to be coming up with weather related one-liners and knock-knock jokes, as soon as they saw the 'rejects' approach. It was all about, 'Oh! Hey Satya, do you know what the weather forecast for tonight is? Dark!' or 'Why are you looking so low? Walking under a rain cloud?' and the like, followed by bellows of laughter leaving no time for her to react. Not like she wanted to react either. Satya knew that reacting would only fuel their mirth. She had developed a sudden deafness, which would surface when bearers of such cheesy jokes appeared anywhere in the newsroom.

Satya was a firm believer of the philosophy that she would not let words hurt her. But seeing Lini and Keerti on-air did not exactly cheer her up. Though anchoring the weather bulletin had not been her idea of a stepping-stone to get to reporting, it still worried her that her goal was nowhere in sight. Rehaan had already chalked up three news reports on the business desk. He was building a reputation as a reporter. She on the other hand, had a slew of production reports and a failed weatherwoman audition.

When would the winds of change blow her way?

9

DESPERATE TRAINEES

'So if you're in Delhi, remember to carry an umbrella as there are plenty of light showers ahead. Back to you Neena…'

'Thanks Keerti and now coming up on the show…'

A split screen showed a cheerful Keerti, making the toss back to Neena, after her weather bulletin. The broad smiles were a must for the anchors to connect with the viewers, they were telecasting to. Yet today it was making one viewer quite prickly and grumpy.

'Oh, reduce the volume on that thing someone,' Satya half-muttered in the general direction of the TV, in the office canteen. She was catching a late dinner of *Alu Parathas* and lime pickle along with slightly sour yoghurt. She had twenty minutes to go, before the office cab guys called her up to tell her that her cab was waiting to drop her back home. Satya was dining with the newsroom's latest couple, Rati and Aniket. Both of them were in the night shift together conveniently, and had come in early for it. It was raining outside, and they had decided to wait out their hour before work with Satya. Satya was usually touched when she saw the lovey-dovey couple. It made her regain faith in humanity and believe in the power of romance and that sort of thing. Today however, she was in too much of a bad mood to cheer up at their cuteness. She had had a bad day.

It had started as most bad days do with her getting out of bed grumpy, thanks to a night interspersed with power cuts, because of a faulty transformer and then she had stubbed her toe. And it was the same toe that she always stubbed when she was in a hurry. And then she had run out of ironed clothes, and thrown on an old but comfortable shirt with jeans. Then every cycle rickshaw she had come across had refused to go to her office, citing a traffic jam in the area. She had finally found a cycle rickshaw with a driver who seemed to resent his job. And Satya had no reasons, to not sympathise with him. After all, at this point she resented her job too. At the office, she had jumped off the rickshaw and managed to catch her shirtsleeve on a metal wire that was poking out from it. It had ripped through the fabric and left a shallow gash on her arm. Annoyed at one of her favourite shirts getting torn and feeling like a hobo in general, Satya had walked into the newsroom, wallowing in self-pity.

Things were not much better there as well. Debashree had pulled her up for reporting twenty minutes late and set her to work immediately. The day's assigned work seemed to be out to get her as well. There had been major audio glitches in a feed in a political story from Pune, and she had scrambled to make it for the nine 'o' clock news. Just as she was running over to the production control room, she had collided with Keerti and almost knocked her over.

'Watch it! Are you blind or something? Oh, it's you Satya! Sorry, you must be running with production work... Ummm... anyway, I have to go to the studio now,' Keerti had said with a tinge of nastiness, as she brushed non-existent lint from her tailored suit, which was bright red for some reason. She had not waited for Satya to respond and had swished her freshly blow-dried hair and walked away. That had been the proverbial last straw on the rotten day Satya had been having so far. Wrapping up her work, she had headed towards the canteen to eat her way out of her misery. Not that the canteen dinner was particularly appetising, but it was free and available at the moment, so Satya had decided to go for it.

The memory of Keerti's patronising tone however, made the bland *Paratha* taste a tad more tasteless. Though she had managed to get through the rest of her shift, with no major train wrecks to speak off, she had ended up in a touchy mood. She felt like she was getting nowhere with her plans to become the best developmental TV reporter the nation had seen. All she was getting was stressed out after the high-powered afternoon shifts, depressed at being stuck behind the scenes, and lonely after watching Rati and Aniket holding hands.

'There is no way this day can get worse,' Satya thought miserably. It was almost like she thought too soon. The day was far from over.

'I was wondering why it's so hot and steamy inside this canteen...and then I see, none other than the sultry Satyabhama Menon, gracing us mere mortals with her heavenly presence! So do you think it's going to continue to rain Satya? Oh, I forgot! You didn't make it as a weatherwoman, did you?'

It was Tina, who seemed to be at her snarly best. Usually she did not sit with Satya for meals, but today it seemed she had her personal agenda in mind. As Rati and Aniket exchanged a hasty look, Tina pulled up a chair and made herself comfortable. Or at least as comfortable as she could be with a mean expression that made her face look even more unpleasant than it usually did.

Tina had wanted to talk to Satya for a while now. It had rankled that she had not been called in for the weatherwoman auditions. She had been stuck in the morning shift, since they had started on the desk. Though she had not been put in the night shift like Satya, she had not created any positive ripples either. She had made it a point to mail Padma all the details about all the work she had put in during the eight hours of every shift she was in office. But Padma was yet to reply to a single one. Tina had given herself six months to move to reporting from the virtual anonymous position of being a desk editor on the general desk. It was September now, seven months to the day they had walked in to the N.E.W.S India newsroom. She was seeking a visibility of some sort. The fact that Satya had gotten an opportunity in the form of an audition, be it after being put through a gruelling night shift, did not make any sense to her. She was sure that Satya had found some secret way to change her destiny from that of a lowly news trainee. And she wanted to be in on it, even if that meant a public fight.

'Give it a break Tina,' Satya snapped back. While she normally gave a patient hearing to most desk editors' frustrated rants, she was in no mood to take Tina's bitterness at the moment. It was not like she was on a personal high herself. Tina however, seemed to be in no mood to back down.

'Intelligence not taking you anywhere Satya? You had to smile at Kedia for a chance at visibility?' she sneered. Satya could feel her temper rising.

'So is that what your close friend Keerti did? So that's how you ace auditions is it? Too bad I didn't know that was the strategy I had to follow!' she flashed back. Tina leaned forward, pushing back her glasses that had slipped down her nose, wisps of hair escaping from her loose ponytail, in her agitation.

'Don't you dare say things about Keerti!' she hissed.

Satya smiled dangerously, 'Oh Ya! I forgot! How could she use her prettiness instead of her brains, when she hardly has any brains right? You're right. I shouldn't have mentioned her… And what about you Tina… You…'

' Stop it! Stop it both of you!'

Rati looked pained. She got up and placed a hand on Satya's shoulder.

'You are both creating a scene. This is stupid and unnecessary. Please stop! Satya, please.' Rati squeezed Satya's shoulder. Satya took a deep breath, gulped down her anger and looked around. The people in the night shift were slowly trickling in. Rain splattered and shaking their raincoats dry, they seemed to be rushing into the dry haven of the canteen. Satya figured that they must have inadvertently raised their voices as she noticed quite a few curious looks being thrown their way.

Tina seemed to have noticed it too. Suddenly she looked like a punctured balloon. She was slightly red-faced as she turned back to Satya. She closed her eyes and slowly moved her head from side to side. She gestured with her hands but remained silent. Then letting out a deep breath, she spoke up, 'Sorry! I don't know what came over me. I was in sector eighteen for dinner. I just headed to office 'cos it started pouring, and I thought I'd catch an office drop back home. I just saw you and it's like something snapped. I mean, at least you are getting an opportunity of some sort you know… For me… It's just so depressing sometimes.' Satya could make out that Tina's apology was sincere.

'I am sorry too for losing my temper Tina. I know what you mean! It's like we've hit rock bottom,' Satya quietly replied. Tina squeezed Satya's hand briefly and walked out of the canteen swiftly. Satya knew that this did not mean that they would become the best of friends from now on, but she could not deny that she felt a sense of empathy with what Tina had been going through. It did not make her feel any better. Satya pushed her plate away. She had lost whatever little appetite she had.

It was a quarter to midnight when she reached home because of the traffic pile-ups due to the rain. Satya knew she had to talk to someone though. She did not want to wake her folks up, so she decided to call someone who she knew would be up at this hour, Rehaan. Even if he was asleep, she knew she could wake him up if need be, that was what they had done in college as well. She rummaged through the freezer and found the carton of chocolate chip ice cream she had bought a week ago. It had melted quite a bit, thanks to her fluctuating power supply, but she was glad to see it there. Taking a generous scoop, she took her phone and curled up on her bed. She took a mouthful dejectedly and pressed two, the speed dial number she had assigned his number to. She listened to his phone ring idly.

'What is taking him so long? Especially when I need to talk!' she thought. And then she heard the phone click yet no one spoke.

Satya spoke up in agitation, 'Rehaan are you asleep? I really need to talk to you! It's been such a bad day...'

And then suddenly, an unfamiliar voice answered, 'Who is this? Why do you want to speak to my son? Are you the girl who is causing trouble?'

Satya was shocked into silence. The irritated voice on the other end though, seemed to have plenty of steam left.

'Hallo? Who is this I asked. This is Rehaan's mother. I am telling you to leave him alone. I have chosen a nice girl for him. We do not want all this love-shove ok? Understand?'

Satya was flabbergasted, for the want of a better word. For a second, Satya considered bursting into tears at the disaster that her day had turned out to be. But then good sense prevailed, and she spoke up, 'Aunty, this is Satya! Rehaan's classmate. I've met you when you came down to our college. I just wanted to speak to him. I'm sorry to be calling so late...'

But nothing she said seemed to be making sense to Rehaan's mum though.

'Oho,' she said with aggression.

'So you've been holding onto him since college *hain*? We are a religious family. We believe in arranged marriage. Please leave him alone. I have selected many beautiful girls for him to choose from. Please do not create a tsunami in our family,' she finished.

While Satya smiled at her choice of words, she felt bad at the trace of the plea she could detect in her voice. She wanted to slap Rehaan for not opening up to his mom. But, judging from the dose, she, a virtual stranger had just received, she was pretty sure that Rehaan's mother would murder him, if he came clean about being gay. As she debated on whether she should try to reason with her or whether she should just hang up, she heard the sound of a scuffle and some rapid Kashmiri being spoken on the other end. Rehaan's voice came on the line.

'Tya, I'm sorry. So, so sorry! Mum's come down for a surprise visit. I'll meet you at your place tomorrow. I need to speak to my mother now. Bye. Sorry!'

He had hung up in a hurry leaving Satya alone to contemplate about how weird her day had been.

The next day Rehaan had given Satya the entire story. His mother had dropped in for a surprise visit, on her way to Mumbai. She had broken her journey in Delhi, only to show Rehaan a couple of snaps of suitable girls, and he had flared up. They had had a massive argument, but he had refused to give her a concrete reason as to why he did not even want to consider the women, she had chosen for him. Satya had been the first female voice to call up after that and she had been unfortunate enough, to become the target of his Mum's ire. She had left for Mumbai by an early morning train and had given Rehaan the ultimatum of a year to come home and get engaged. Happy at having vented to Satya and having gotten a year's time to come out of the closet, Rehaan was back to normal again. It was now Satya's turn to unload. She started off by giving him a blow-by-blow account, of how awful her day had been. It was Rehaan's turn to play patient listener.

'I cannot believe that Tina and I were bonding about scraping the bottom of the barrel'

Satya was only half-speaking to Rehaan. They were having Chinese food at her apartment again. She had her weekly off while Rehaan had come in straight from work for their weekly session. Though Chinese was Satya's all time favourite comfort food, this time it did not seem to be doing its job as well as it usually did. Dressed in her comfortable old pyjamas, Satya was sitting cross-legged on the floor, distractedly twirling noodles on to her plastic fork. She had never quite figured chopsticks out. Rehaan however, was shovelling the food into his mouth, at break neck speed. That meant he was fine and happy with life and had already let the previous day's incidents go. He only tended to dawdle over food when he was pre-occupied.

'Hmmm…' He said, as Satya whined about the rut she seemed to be in. Satya was not very happy about her best friend's reaction.

'Hmmm? That's the best you can do? Can you be slightly more

supportive, maybe? You know, considering I was nice enough to be supportive of the way you are hiding stuff from your poor mother!' she asked in an icy tone.

'You know what? I think you are where you are, because you're not showing any initiative!' Rehaan gave the chewing a rest, as he reacted to Satya's sharp tone. Satya was taken aback.

'Are you trying to pick a fight or something Rehaan? 'Cos I'll have you know that I'm more than ready for it!' Satya snarled, as she carefully placed her fork onto her plate. Rehaan could see that she was getting ready for an argument.

'Ok, ok before you bite my head off, listen to me,' Rehaan laid his fork down on his plate, swallowed the morsel he had in his mouth and switched off the T.V, to emphasise how serious he was.

'See, you do a great job at the desk. So your bosses are impressed. But they do not know that you want to report right? So they see you producing excellent stories, and making great headlines. How are they supposed to know that this is not what you want to do, right? It's not like you are bombarding them with story ideas or critiquing reporters. Like me for example, how do you think I get these opportunities to report? I keep bombarding the business desk with emails and once in a while I mail Nandan, saying I think this angle should have been covered or that there was too much *masala* in this one… It's not like they need to take my opinion into consideration or ever will, but then at least I'm letting them know that I have an opinion! You know what I mean? Let them know that you're interested in reporting, that you have a flair for it…'

Satya was silent as she thought about what Rehaan had blurted out. A slow smile dawned over Satya's face.

'You know that actually makes sense.'

She picked up her fork again. Her appetite was returning. She speared a piece of garlic chicken on her fork and smiled at Rehaan.

'That actually makes sense,' she repeated. Now that Satya had the first glimmer of a forward plan, she was more than ready to talk about something else. They completed the rest of the dinner, reminiscing about good old college days and occasionally lapsing into updating each other on office gossip.

The next day, it was with a light step that Satya clambered on to a cycle rickshaw, as she took one on her way to office. She had decided to act on Rehaan's words.

'Initiative, that's what I need to show!' she resolutely thought. Jolting her out of her determined thoughts, Satya's phone rang out to the tone of a desk phone.

'How come *Amma*'s calling now?' she wondered, as she recognised the caller tone.

'Hello *Amma*,' she trilled into the phone with all the enthusiasm, she was feeling at the newly created "take initiative" plan.

'Hello and how is my soon to be famous reporter today? Still getting irritated by the weather cracks?'

Satya's mother's warm voice flowed through the connection, and seemed to envelop Satya in a bear hug.

'I am fine today Amma. I am completely over what happened day before yesterday. It was just another bad day, that's all. Right now, I'm on my way to office, with a plan with a Capital P, like they say in the bank heist movies'

Satya replied, picturing her mum on the other end of the line. She was probably sitting on the sofa in the sitting room, wearing a comfortable *salwar kameez*, with her legs stretched out in front of her, propped up on the low coffee table. She usually called a little later in the day. She must have some news today.

'So I wanted to ask you something…' Ambika Menon started off.

'And there it is,' Satya thought. She remained silent waiting for her mother to go on.

'It's Devyani's wedding on September 30th right? Do you think you can make it? 'Cos most of our families will be coming in from everywhere. So it will be a great way for you to catch up with everyone…' She trailed off waiting for her daughter's reply.

Satya was hesitant in replying, 'Hmmm, I don't know *Amma*… That's like three weeks away and…'

'Yes, but its been so long since I saw you and you can dress up traditionally.' Ambika tried to persuade her.

'Exactly, I'll have to dress up and all… But on the other hand, I have not taken any of my leaves yet and they might lapse… Hmmm, let me ask Padma today'

Satya could hear her mother's glee as she responded.

'Oh great! I'll let you go about your work now. I'll be waiting to hear from you. Bye Sweetie, Love you'

'Love you, too Amma. I'll call you as soon as I hear from Padma, ok? Bye.'

'Maybe, I should go home. It will be a welcome change and I can start with my "take initiative" strategy on a fresh slate,' Satya reflected as she hung up.

The newsroom was bustling with energy, but fortunately for Satya, it was the normal amount of activity that took place every day. There was no breaking news situation at present, so comparatively speaking it was a good time to approach the heads of the news desk. Even then, it was with a certain amount of nervousness, that Satya approached Padma. She seemed unusually hyperactive and frustrated today. Her short hair was in disarray, presumably because of the number of times she had run her hands through them. She was running her fingers through her hair as Satya approached her too.

'Ummm Padma, can I have a minute?' Satya started hesitantly.

'Why not? All of you just want my time today, don't you!' Padma snapped uncharacteristically. Satya was thrown and got a mental image of her vacation being flushed down the drain. But she knew she had to give it a shot for her mental satisfaction, and also because Padma was looking at her waiting for her to continue. Satya gulped down the sudden panic in her throat and went on.

'Well… actually… I just wanted to ask you if…' She started off.

'Ask me what?' Padma was practically barking now.

'Demand that you get transferred to reporting like your friend

Tina? Make a fuss about being stuck editing and producing stories, while you'd rather be a celeb on–air. What is it that you too want to ask me Satya?'

'So that's what this is all about! Oh I wish I could slap Tina for doing this. There is no way I can start with my reporting strategy like this. Damn her!' Satya mentally cursed Tina. Judging by the state Padma was in, forget going on a vacation, Satya felt like she would now be condemned to years and years of production. And weirdly enough, Padma seemed to be more hurt than angry by Tina's request. She was behaving like a mauled lioness.

Satya cautiously tread her way through, 'Actually I just wanted to know if I could avail of my leaves for the last week of September and the first week of November. My cousin's getting married. And my leaves lapse in December…' Satya stopped, uncertain of how to continue.

Padma looked at her for a minute and then gave her an unsure smile. She ran her fingers through her hair one more time, but they seemed to have lost the manic energy they had been possessed by. Padma then gave Satya her characteristic searching look and said, 'Oh…is that it? In that case, mail me the dates and let me see,' she smiled dismissively and turned back to her monitor.

Satya now had enough reason to remain distracted while she worked. Through out the shift, Satya had opened every mail of Padma's with anticipation. They had all turned out to be work related messages. In her characteristic style, Padma had opted to keep Satya dangling on tenterhooks. It was only when Satya was wrapping up that the mail had come in.

"Your leave has been approved.

Keep up the good work.

Padma"

The mail was calm. Padma seemed like she was back to her normal self. Satya quickly replied with a 'thank you' mail and rushed out of the newsroom to call her mother. Though she had been indecisive initially, now she was excited about the prospect of holidaying with her family. It would be a refreshing change.

The two weeks before the vacation passed, with lots of shopping before and after shifts, and discussions about the shopping, during the breaks in the shifts. Satya needed at least two outfits and Rati was the best person to go with. She could bargain, till the shopkeepers jaw dropped. Rati and Satya headed to Connaught Place for picking up wedding related attire and ended up discovering a wonderland with all sorts of shops to choose from. They headed to the fashion lover's favourite street market Janpath at nine in the morning, to bargain with stall owners as soon as they opened shop. This got them the best bargains and also the outfits that had not been pawed at by other aggressive shoppers. Rati was at her haggling best at Chandni Chowk too, where they scanned the streets for matching accessories. Stones of varied sizes and colours glinted at them from the sidewalk where they were displayed. Satya found herself slipping into a world where kings still ruled their princely states and decking oneself up was a way of life. She could almost catch the whiffs of bygone eras in the crooked lanes of Old Delhi. She could picture women clad in fantastical muslin clothes gliding past, while colourful strangers passed the streets carried in palanquins or borne by mules and horses.

In a nutshell, she was useless as a shopper, and if it had not been for Rati, she would probably have ended up wearing something old or borrowed to the wedding. Rati wasted no time in slipping into the past, and kept her focus. She held her street sense firmly in her hands and supervised the craftsmen who were nimbly stringing the stones and beads into necklaces and earrings, at an agreed upon price. Once Rati had done the once-over of all of Satya's new acquisitions, she was finally ready. Packing done, gifts purchased and with a promise of a packet of banana chips for Aniket, a Kerala sari for Rati and a *Kathakali* figurine for Rehaan, Satya was off.

She got a window seat as always. She peered at Delhi, as the flight lifted itself from the nation's capital. She found it weird that she did not even feel a twinge of heartache, as she left the city that had been her home for seven months now. While she loved Old Delhi, her brain refused to accept NOIDA as a place where she could spread her roots. She always felt like she was in transit, even when she was in her apartment. A feeling of living out of a suitcase, even when she was fully unpacked. Glad to leave it all behind for a period of two-weeks, she leaned back and relaxed. She could afford to doze off, it was a low-cost flight and there was no danger of being woken up by the airhostess with food, freebies or even cotton balls for her ears.

It was the pilot's announcement that woke her up a couple of hours later. They were beginning their descent to Kochi airport. Satya pulled the window blind up and gazed outside. The flight was losing altitude fast and an entire region of green seemed to be rising up, to meet the plane with great speed. As she watched, the specks transformed themselves into houses, people and cars. The grey lines amidst the green became the city's highways. And the rich patches of green, the coconut trees Kerala was so famous for. As the plane prepared to land, Satya braced herself.

'It's great to be back home!' she thought.

10

THE BACHELORETTE

Satya walked towards the arrival gate, taking in deep breaths of the humid yet fresh air of the state that she called her home. The state that lived up to its clichéd reputation of being God's own country — Kerala. It was rejuvenating to breathe in air, which was free from dust and had a strong feel of nature in it. Though it was probably psychological, Satya could feel her pent up stress fall away from her, with every step. She picked her baggage up from the slightly worn out conveyor belt that seemed to be groaning under the weight of the passengers' personal belongings. She checked whether the bag was indeed hers as there were many other identical ones that were continuing on their joy ride, unclaimed. Once she made sure that it was definitely hers, she hoisted it on to the trolley and walked towards the exit on the far end of the airport. As she looked intently at the crowds with placards, waiting for their loved ones on the other side of the arrival gate, she could see her parents peering in through the glass doors. Pushing her trolley, she half-walked, half-ran out to be caught up in a bear hug. It was her father who was now beaming at her. Wordlessly he pressed a Cadbury's Fruit and Nut bar into her hand.

'Oho, Dad! I am twenty-three years old now! You always give me chocolates when I come home!' Satya said with a wide smile, completely contradicting her words as she hastily tore open the wrapper and started wolfing the bar down.

'That's 'cos for me, you are always my itty-bitty daughter' he said in his deep voice, as he ruffled her hair. Her mother, who was standing next to him, also gave her a tight hug.

'Welcome home sweetie! We missed you,' she said, giving her the routine motherly once-over. She looked pleased at what she saw, as she did not make any of her typical, "You've lost weight or gained weight or what have you done to your hair," type of comments. Satya's dad who had plucked her bag from her hands, was now almost by the car and gesturing at them to follow him. As she held onto her mum's hand tightly and walked swiftly towards the car, Satya felt warm inside. The coconut trees were swaying, there was scrumptious chocolate in her belly, no reports waiting to be edited, no scrambling around thinking of what to eat for the next meal of the day. Just home and family and relaxing and sleeping late! Just thinking about her lazy days ahead made her smile broadly. Satya put her feet up on the back seat and curled up with a cushion behind her back. The ride to her home from the airport, would take at least forty-five minutes. Plenty of time, to start talking about the life she had been leading in NOIDA.

She started to fill in her parents about the workings of the huge channel she was a part of. It was good to ramble on, without having to worry about long distance phone bills. It was good to see her parents' expressions, as she narrated incident after incident. From the "tape monster" to the "whoreships", she made sure that she left nothing out even though she had mentioned them on the phone earlier. She had just started on Menaka and the hag that she was, when her mother spoke up, a tad hesitantly.

'Oh by the way, I forgot to mention. Please do not get mad or think about it and sulk in advance ... but... but ... okay, so Sita Aunty will be there at the wedding. And she has apparently been telling everyone that she wants to meet you...'

Her mother looked away quickly, after delivering her news. There was a dumbstruck silence from the back seat and then a sudden outburst.

'What! Sita Aunty? The Sita Aunty from Palakkad! Why does she want to see me? Who has she been telling that she wants to see me?' Satya exclaimed.

And then a sudden suspicion crept in.

'Oh no! Oh no, no, no! I'm this time's target, aren't I? So this was a set up! You knew that if you mentioned her I would never ever come. Why *Amma*? And Dad? I never thought you would also stand by plots like these!'

Her tone of righteous indignation rang out loudly in the car, as her parents stared steadfastly ahead, pointedly trying to ignore Satya, whose gaze now seemed to be boring into the backs of their heads.

'This is not happening, ok!' Satya announced as she crossed her arms with a mulish expression on her face.

Her dad spoke up in his soothing voice, 'Satya, your mother has been making up excuses to avoid her calls. We had nothing to do with this. We just wanted to see you. It's been a while and we miss you. And we knew that if we gave you a heads- up about her while you were in Delhi, you might not have come. That was the only reason why we didn't…'

Satya cut in with a contrite expression, 'Sorry Dad! I just lost it thinking of Sita Aunty and her ways. And I would have of course come anyway, if you guys had told me you were missing me *na*? It's just that you know how she is *na*…'

Of course, they did. Her parents nodded forcefully in unison as they too were thinking about the personality that was Sita Aunty.

"The aunt from hell!" That's how Satya and her cousins had referred to Sita Aunty for as long as they could remember. Plump, always swathed in expensive silk saris in loud colours, her hair in a neat bun with jasmine flowers encircling it and a big red bindi that completed her look. Sita Aunty was a permanent fixture at all places where more than ten members of Satya's mother's family met. At family get-togethers, when Satya and her cousins were kids, Sita Aunty was the one who told them to sit up straight, and comb their hair when they were busy rough housing or telling the girls to dress appropriately and favouring the boys over them. She had never been popular with the women of the family and this dislike spanned across all the generations, right from Satya's grandmother to her youngest cousin.

Sita Aunty's daughters too had very low ratings on the family popularity index. They were prim and proper and used to behave like stereotypical middle-aged old women even when they were in their teens. Not surprising, considering the control freak they had for their mother, Satya had once sympathetically thought as she saw them sit far away from the semi-violent dodge ball game she and her cousins were playing. Characteristically, Sita Aunty had married off both her daughters to wealthy businessmen in the Gulf, within a year of each other. The sisters had barely entered their twenties, when the big fat arranged Indian weddings had taken place. Many in the family had privately remarked, rather snidely that the daughters had probably agreed to early marriages, just to get away from their overbearing mother. Everyone seemed to concur on that one.

Now, with nothing much to do, apart from calling the couples up to enquire about when they planned to give her grandchildren, Sita Aunty had made herself the self-proclaimed wedding arranger, for the rest of the family, sometimes even for friends of the family or distant acquaintances. Her mission these days was to marry off every boy and girl in Satya's large but tightly knit family, as soon as they reached the 'eligible' age in her opinion. And the 'eligible' age according to her was?

'Well if they are old enough to vote for someone to govern the country, then I think they are old enough to manage a family. But boys, probably need to be a little older. Maybe twenty four or twenty five?' Suffice to say, these oft repeated words had not increased her popularity amongst Satya's cousins, both male and female.

In terms of actual relations, she was Satya's mother's third cousin but she behaved like she was her mother. She had been indirectly referring to 'eligible' girls being let loose for more than two or three years, at every wedding when she was within Satya's mum's earshot. Satya herself had not attended a wedding in the family for more than four years now. She had been away at college and this was the first time, she would be meeting up with her extended family after getting a job. She had landed in Kerala with ideas of showing off her new clothes, and impressing her younger cousins with stories of her living alone and being part of the making of the news. And also stories of meeting celebrities! Though till now, the only celebrity she had met was the younger brother of a famous film star, who had acted in a few flop movies and then moved to theatre. She had seen him outside her office, waiting to pick up his girlfriend who worked with the N.E.W.S India online division. She had considered throwing in a few white lies about her work as well, just to see the wide-eyed look of admiration in her cousins' eyes. But the prospect of meeting Sita Aunty, threw a dampener on it all. Yet she decided to grin and bear it, for if she stewed over it through the two weeks she had, she was not very sure when she would get another break any time soon.

There was a week to go before the wedding celebrations began. The phone lines had been buzzing with all the calls about the kinds of outfits and jewellery that everyone had picked up for the event. It was like the family could not wait for the festivities to begin. *Malayali* weddings were traditionally short affairs, with a five-minute ceremony followed by a sumptuous multiple course meal or a *sadhya* as it was called. This time though, there was a family get-together planned the day before the wedding, so that everyone could meet and catch up, before the wedding madness began. For the girls of the family, it was just an excuse to show off a pretty outfit. Satya was looking forward to this. She had relatives who were journalists and apart from catching up, she figured this would also be a great time to network and make a few contacts. This was the only time that would be possible as the wedding would be too chaotic. But before anything wedding related happened, she had the serious business of relaxing to get down to and that's precisely what she had been doing at home.

Satya had been enjoying the pampering she was now accorded to at home, due to her 'guest faculty' status. There were no chores as used to be the case, when she stayed at home. On the contrary, she was like the special guest, who got to decide the menu for the day. Her mother did not seem to be complaining just yet. And so, Satya set about shamelessly taking full advantage of her new, elevated status, asking her mother for all her favourite dishes. She knew she had to soak up as much of the relaxation as possible before the relatives started trickling in, from various parts of the country and abroad. She was determined to make the most of this vacation. So what if she would be sacrificial lamb number one, to be slaughtered at Sita Aunty's altar once the party started. There were six entire days before that happened. And it was time to sit down in front of the TV, sleep late, stuff oneself with delicious Amma made food and generally luxuriate in the bliss that was home.

The eve of the party finally dawned. Dressed in a lilac and gold chiffon sari, Satya was deep in conversation with her cousin.

'I think I've put on weight in the six days that I've been home,' Satya was telling Radhika, her cousin and closest friend in the family. They were helping themselves to yet another portion of the chicken kebabs that were being passed around liberally at the dinner party.

Just a couple of years apart in age, Satya and Radhika were as close as sisters and even shared their sun signs. Radhika was Ambika's sister's daughter, and she had come home for the wedding too. She was at college in Bangalore, studying public relations. As kids, she and Satya had had joint birthday parties and even worn the same kind of clothes. Even though their dressing styles had diversified over the years, they were still on the exact same wavelength and managed to finish each other's sentences, as they used to when they were children.

'Ya, I know what you mean. It's so cool to come home after a gap. Mum's been expressing how much she misses me through her cooking too…'

Radhika replied as she dipped the kebab in mint chutney.

'That certainly won't help you both when the marriage proposals come your way,' rasped a gruff but feminine voice behind them. Exchanging a trapped look, the cousins turned to face their worst nightmare in person.

'Hello Sita Aunty,' they chanted in unison, with gloom writ across their pretty faces. Sita Aunty was surveying them with much the same expression, as a spider would look at helpless flies. Dressed in a trademark *Kancheepuram* sari of flame Orange with a gold border, Sita Aunty was looking at Satya and Radhika with deep interest. It was up to the cousins to make the next move and both of them were thinking on their feet. Radhika however decided that each of them was on their own as far as the natural disaster called Sita Aunty was concerned. She suddenly waved at someone over Sita Aunty's shoulder and rapidly called out.

'What? Right now? But I'm having a conversation with Sita Aunty... Ok if you insist...Ok, ok I'm coming!'

She turned towards Sita with an obviously fake apologetic smile.

'Ummm, I think Devayani needs something, I'll be right back.'

Satya knew that Radhika was just making a hasty escape and that there was no way that Sita Aunty would see her anywhere for the rest of the day. She knew she had to make an attempt too.

'Oh do you think she will need me too? Why don't I come with you?' Satya asked with false earnestness and just a hint of desperation.

Radhika gave her a wicked grin and replied, 'No Tya. If you also come with me, then poor Sita Aunty will not have anyone to talk to *na*! And then she might also feel like coming and helping out Devu with whatever she needs. I think you should just stay here and give her company. I will be back soon'

With that Radhika hurried away, leaving Satya alone with Sita Aunty. Satya knew when to give up, but she made a mental note to give Radhika a piece of her mind when they were alone. At a safe distance from Sita Aunty and Satya, Radhika turned, grinned and mouthed a 'Sorry' and then merged in, amongst the fineries that were thronging the room. Now that Radhika had beaten Satya to the 'Oh – someone's – calling- me- move' and dumped her in her last ditch attempt to escape, Satya was well and truly trapped.

Resigned to her fate, she proffered Sita Aunty a small smile. Sita Aunty smiled back, as if she had been waiting for the drama to get over, so that she could start with the piece she had kept ready, ever since she had heard that Satya would be attending the wedding.

'So Satyabhama how is Delhi? I always found it too cold. I've gone there with Uncle you know,' Sita Aunty started off, while taking immense care to clutch on to Satya's hand as if to prevent her sole victim from escaping. Satya was pleasantly surprised.

'Wow! She's off the wedding topic for a change,' Satya thought as she allowed herself to be steered to a chair away from the kebabs.

'He took me to the Taj Mahal on our honeymoon... So romaaantic,' she simpered, as she gave Satya a sidelong glance. Satya realised that she had hoped, but in vain.

'Oh no! Here we go,' Satya thought as a waiter passed in front of her, with succulent chicken kebabs. She took a longing look towards the platter and let out an almost inaudible sigh. She unwillingly wrenched her attention back to Sita Aunty's droning.

'You know, a job is something you can get at any point in your life, but once you cross your marriageable age, you will remain alone with all the money. What do you think of that?'

As if on cue, images of diving into and somersaulting in a vault full of money, flashed through Satya's head. Shaking her head slightly, Satya dismissed them and decided to apply logic in the face of annoying irrationality.

'That's not such a bad thing Aunty. But see for me the thing is, that sooner or later I will start reporting, and then I'll be on call twenty-four hours and so I won't have time for anyone else, least of all a husband. And also I know so many people that haven't gotten married and are perfectly happy. So there is really no need for all the marriage business is there?' Satya argued.

'Oh no!' Sita Aunty rolled her eyes dramatically looking up at the ceiling, and the corners of her mouth drooped theatrically. For all the histrionics, Satya knew that the look of despair on Sita Aunty's face was genuine. She was one of those who believed seriously, that everyone who hits marriageable age must get hitched as soon as possible, lest they corrupt coming generations. Satya was not sure whether she could handle this on her own. She looked around the room desperately, waiting for the slightest eye contact from someone. She wanted to abandon this conversation and above all this infuriating woman at the slightest flicker of a friendly eye. But it seemed to her, that all her cousins were looking in the other direction deliberately. Even those relatives who were moving across the room to catch up and converse with everyone, seemed to quicken their pace when they neared or crossed Satya's little corner of doom. They knew that to rescue Satya was to give their selves up to her fate. And frankly, no one was interested. Earning Satya's ire and wrath the next day, seemed to be more than a fair price for avoiding Sita Aunty.

Unmindful of Satya's desperation, Sita Aunty continued, 'I've talked to your mother and she has been telling me that you are busy with your work, so I shouldn't bother about you. But you, Satya, are a burden on these very shoulders of mine.'

She finished by patting each of her shoulders with a flourish. By this time, Satya had begun to realise that there was no point in getting angry. She let Sita Aunty continue with her preaching. The latter justified, 'You see, even though you don't know you are unhappy, I know that you will be. So I have been making enquiries just for you. I tried to tell your mother, but she has been very busy everytime, I called her. I couldn't manage to get through to her.'

Satya could imagine her poor mother frantically pulling out excuses from the top of her head, to avoid having to deal with this unsolicited matrimonial help. Satya knew that the entire process would be quicker if she gave in and let Sita Aunty go on with her plans and ideas. If she escaped that would just mean Sita Aunty would stalk her and go over the entire conversation again and again, till she, her mother, her father and even her grandmother were part of the grand plan.

'I might as well get over with this before the wedding tomorrow. That way, I won't have to spend the entire day finding ways to escape from this woman's clutches,' Satya thought resignedly. She stopped fidgeting and scanning the room for knights or heroic damsels in shiny silks and turned towards Sita Aunty.

'So what do you propose Aunty?'

Sita Aunty looked pleased at Satya's sudden interest.

'Well, I have these lovely proposals… I have a picture of yours from a family get together long ago, and that's what I showed these people,' she said with the confident smile of a conspirator who was happy at things going according to plan. Satya heaved a sigh of relief.

She knew that any picture of hers from more than three years ago would drive any self-respecting traditional family away. She was going through her punk phase back then, with a steel nose ring, spiked up hair and deep blue nail colour. Taking her grin for acquiescence, Sita Aunty continued proudly, 'Also whenever I meet a suitable boy, I tell them to watch your channel, so that they can hear your voice.'

'Well, at least N.E.W.S India can boast of increased ratings, thanks to my matrimonial alliances,' Satya thought wryly.

Sita Aunty went on, 'So there's this nice family, son is in America, researching on different kinds of parasites…'

'Ummm Aunty, I can't leave India. So assuming that I agree to listen to you, you have to cut out all the boys outside India, ok?' Satya intercepted.

'Not even the Gulf?'

Sita Aunty was wide-eyed at what seemed to her as the strangest criteria, any girl from Kerala, the NRI's own country, would ever put forward.

'Especially not the Gulf,' Satya reiterated, 'Also it should be preferably someone in the media,' she added.

'Oh! You have criteria and all… One minute, do you have … a… boyfriend? Is that why you have all this criteria? So that we never find someone you like and then you can marry your… your boyfriend instead?'

Sita Aunty made the word 'boyfriend' sound like a dirty word, the kind one should never utter in public. She was looking at Satya accusingly, a tiny frown wrinkling her already not so smooth brow.

'No, no Aunty. It's just that if you are so determined to arrange it, then you might as well arrange it to the last detail *na*?' Satya replied with a straight face, patting herself on the back mentally for keeping her composure, while having one of the weirdest conversations of her life. And for uttering sentences that she had never thought, would come out of her mouth.

Sita Aunty looked convinced. She went on, 'Hmmm, that is true. So no boys outside India, that reduces the number of boys I have considerably… Oh I almost forgot, there was one boy in Mumbai, I think he works for a bank or something. He is uncle's brother's wife's cousin's son… But the person I liked was the boy's mother. She was very happy that you work for a news channel. She was very interested in your job.'

'Oh?' Satya was surprised and intrigued, 'Wow! So she likes TV journalism and reporters and stuff?' she asked with interest.

Sita Aunty explained, 'Actually, she kept on repeating that she was very happy that you work for a private news channel. She was saying, that her son would be very pleased about it too. She was saying that if the girl works for a news channel, her provident fund would be sizeable after retirement. So it makes good sense to marry her son off to a girl like you.'

Satya could not believe what she had just heard. Unsure of whether to laugh or launch into a lecture, she opted for an incredulous 'What!' that came out as a squeak instead. She cleared her throat and tried again.

'So…let me get this straight…She likes me as a possible bride for her son who works for a bank or something of the sort, because I have the potential to work my life away at a news channel so that they can collect my provident fund, once I have retired?'

Sita Aunty looked at her with a puzzled expression as if Satya was asking a tricky question. She considered it for a while before answering cautiously.

'Yes?'

Confirmation. That was all Satya needed. She felt like she was stuck in a B-grade soap opera. There were beautiful people dressed in wonderful clothes around her. The hall was decorated to resemble a movie set. And she was having a conversation with a woman, who had the audacity to propose to her, an idea about getting married to a guy, whose mother seemed to like her already, but only for the money she might earn or save. And on another note, God knew that there was no money. Satya got up, turned and faced Sita Aunty. She opened her mouth and then shut it again without saying anything. She moved her head from side to side. And walked away with a smile on her face.

'You actually left her sitting there?'

Radhika asked disbelievingly, while sputters of laughter escaped her. She was staying over at Satya's house for the night. They were both upstairs in Satya's room, huddled on the bed. Satya grinned in the darkness. It was past three in the morning they had been gossiping all night, ignoring the fact that they had to wake up early for the wedding the next day. Talking through the night was something they had done as kids, and weddings or other events were not likely to change it. Though they had talked about the abandoning of Sita Aunty, many, many times now, they kept returning to the topic.

'Yup! I just left her sitting there and I walked away. I didn't even turn back. I walked through the hall, I found Amma and told her the entire conversation right away. She laughed so hard that she had tears in her eyes. I got worried, 'cos I thought people would think I had been yelling at her or something. Anyway I told her that I would be ignoring Sita Aunty from now on, of course, she agreed.'

'I can imagine.' Radhika giggled.

'Ya, though it sounds funny now, I was pissed off then you know. She makes it sound like a business, like I am a cow or a prize calf or something. I hope she blacklists me for my rude behaviour now. The less I have to do with her, the better it will be for the both of us.'

Satya declared with a smile, as she plumped up her pillow and lay down.

'I am so glad that I am not in her special spotlight yet!' Radhika muttered, flopping down on her side of the bed.

'Ya, ya, I'm next in line! I heard that from about twenty people today,' Satya grumbled good-naturedly.

'I have half a mind to skip attending the wedding tomorrow and head for a movie instead.'

'You wouldn't!' Radhika gasped.

'No, I wouldn't. I have a new outfit to show off,' Satya replied drolly.

Radhika smiled and rubbed her eyes sleepily. Satya lay silently for a while. She could hear a cricket chirping away persistent for its mate. There was a light breeze and the curtains were moving, as if they had a life of their own. Each time they flew up, a little bit of moonlight flitted into the room, making shadows on the walls.

'All the marriage talk makes me want to find a boyfriend, just to keep the vultures off me…' Satya whispered.

'Oh, that's so dumb!' Radhika mumbled, half asleep.

'Ya, but still, anything to get them off it. I mean, I agree that my job can be tedious at times. But I love being independent and I like my time with my space and myself. I like coming home after a hectic shift and finding peace and quiet in my apartment. You know what I mean Radhi? … Radhi?'

Radhika grunted in her sleep. Satya pulled the covers over her and turned to the other side. She lay lost in her thoughts.

The search seemed to be far from over for the cricket though. He was still chirping as Satya fell asleep.

11

BLIND DATE

'Oh yum, these must be the best banana chips in the world,' said a very happy Aniket as he grabbed a handful from the packet on Satya's desk. She was back in office, cheerful and relaxed in a white shirt paired up with a thick jacket and jeans. She was perched on her swivel chair, occasionally checking her PC, looking happy at having goodies to hand out to her friends. Aniket was chomping away with enthusiasm, after stashing away the half kg packet that Satya had brought exclusively for him safely in his satchel. Satya smiled at him as she cleared the flotsam and jetsam kind of emails that had ended up in her inbox, over the two weeks that she had been away.

It had not been easy to leave home, especially after the two weeks of precious leave that had seemed to fly away. At the airport she had clung to her parents for a while, feeling like a child being pushed off to boarding school. It was the prospect of returning to friends like Rehaan, Rati and Aniket that had made it a tad easier. Halfway through the flight, she had actually found herself looking forward to getting back.

'Who knows?' She thought, 'What if they realised what an asset I was in my absence and decided to move me to reporting? Now that's a happy thought. It's possible isn't it?'

No such luck. It was true that she had been missed as proven by the wide smiles of her friends and their tight hugs. But unfortunately, her big bosses did not seem to have registered her absence. Satya was back in the afternoon shift, as she had been from the beginning, save the night shift ordeal. But today she had no complaints. It was a Saturday and it was also a slow news day. Weekends were the days when the maximum number of recorded shows played, which meant that work was negligible. So there was a lot of free time for the four friends to catch up. A new café had opened in the office lobby downstairs and Rati along with Rehaan had gone off to get cappuccinos for the four of them, to enjoy with the banana chips. Something they would have never been able to do, had it been a weekday.

The newsroom atmosphere was laid back today. The head honchos almost never came in on the weekends, if it was a slow news day. The mice were definitely at play, when the top cats were away. Most of the people on the shift were taking self-imposed coffee breaks and some of the TV's in the newsroom were playing music channels. However there were those, whose duties were not affected by the weekend. Today Sunil was amongst those sad souls. Poor Sunil who was stuck in front of the ticker, was left staring at the screen. Come rain or shine, weekday or weekend, nothing changed for the person who was manning the ticker. A sympathetic Satya had left him a pile of chips to munch on, while he remained the only person who had no option but to be true to his duty.

Rati and Rehaan returned with the steaming hot cappuccinos and the four arranged their swivel chairs to face each other. Sunil looked longingly at the four of them for a second, before he turned back to the ticker. The four of them made sympathetic noises for Sunil and then they shrugged and got back to catching up with each other.

Rehaan raised his glass and said with genuine emotion, 'To Satya, for bringing me a Kathakali figurine, these wonderful banana chips and most all, for coming back'

Satya chuckled and raised her glass. Aniket laughed and added, 'Yes, we were placing bets on whether you would come back to this place and your best friend here was the only one who thought you would. Even my beautiful girlfriend was not all that sure when we didn't hear from you'

Rati slapped his wrists at this point and shook her head vociferously as if to say that Aniket was exaggerating as usual. Satya smiled at the two of them.

'Awww, girlfriend and boyfriend and all… you guys are the cutest. But in my defence, I didn't have time to check mail *na* people. I was with my folks and my cousin and I am not sure when I'll get my next vacation. So I wanted to make sure that I was with them one hundred percent. Is that justification enough?' Satya asked, as she smiled at the lot of them.

'Ya, ya, give your excuses later. First tell me how the wedding was and what people thought of your outfits.' Rati cut in.

'Oh the wedding was beautiful. There were around a hundred guests and beautiful floral decorations and Devyani, my cousin who got married, wore this awesome deep pink sari with gold embroidery. Of course, everyone loved my clothes, especially the accessories! I told them that you had a major hand in me getting them at these prices. Now some of them want to come to Delhi to shop, before the next major event in the family, which a lot of them hope is my wedding! But then I politely informed them that, they would have to wait a long time for that to happen! Anyway, I don't have the photos of the functions yet, but I will show them to you guys as soon as I get them mailed to me…and then oh, one of my aunts came up with this bizarre wedding proposal. Someone's mother liking me 'cos I might be a good source of money after my retirement and some such nonsense! I think I will have to take a leaf out of your book Rehaan and spread a rumour that I'm gay or something to make the proposals stop. Anyway, I've decided that I'll be attending no more family weddings, till I find a boyfriend. So, you tell me what's up with you guys? What's been happening around here?'

Satya waited to hear Rati's response with interest.

'*Yaar*, even my relatives have been bugging me with photographs of eligible bachelors and inane proposals. No need to sulk Aniket, I will be calling up my mother and updating her about us really soon,'

Rati said in a consolatory tone to Aniket who had looked crestfallen. After making sure that her boyfriend was all cheered up, Rati went on in a slightly more conspiratorial tone.

'Anyway, what's really happening here is that someone has been ensuring top female attendance in the newsroom.'

'Huh?' Satya looked at the four uncomprehendingly.

'What? Like there's a discriminatory female attendance system? 'Cos that's totally illegal!' Satya said, her journalistic senses aroused by Rati's hush - hush tone.

'Uff oh! No, no, nothing like that! Switch tracks. Think on our level yaar,' Rati half turned her body and tilted her head slightly in the general direction of the sports desk. Aniket let out a mock exasperated breath, rolled his eyes and muttered, 'I don't think he's all that great!' The slight envy that came through in his delivery seemed to tell a different story though.

'What are you guys talking about?'

Satya looked confused. She looked around the newsroom vaguely and still could not figure out what her friends were going on and on about.

'Satya, why don't you just look at the direction in which I'm pointing? See Satya look in the direction I'm gesturing at with my head! Come on don't be so frikking dumb! Just open your eyes and look *na*!'

Rati was now mumbling quite agitatedly at Satya's apparent inability to follow direction. Satya was totally flummoxed. She now peered past Rati's head and saw what Rati was pointing at.

'The sports desk? What happened to the sports desk? Is it a new desk? Do they have new edit machines? What is it?'

It was Rehaan's turn to get exasperated now.

'For God's sake! Not what, you foolish girl! Who, who at the sports desk? That's what you should be asking! What it seems!'

He finished off, by hitting his forehead with his hand, quite forcefully to emphasise his exasperation at Satya's obtuseness. Intrigued by Rati and Rehaan's mysterious but persistent behaviour and Aniket's constant eye rolling, Satya stood right up to get a clear view of the mysterious presence on the sports desk. Rati watched as she saw the confusion on her face clear.

'Oh!' she said. 'Of course! Why didn't I notice before? Hey!' she shouted out and waved. Rati and Rehaan exchanged a curious look. That was certainly not the reaction they had expected. Satya went on waving, unmindful of her friends' surprise.

'Hey! Hey Shanks, come over here! I just got back from Kerala and I've brought banana chips from home… I just … I just … Ohhhh!'

Rehaan and Rati looked at each other with broad smiles.

'And now, she sees!' they chanted in unison. Satya was standing with her hand raised in a half wave, in a trance of sorts, staring at the sports desk. Though this time, she was staring at someone at the sports desk and not just the sports desk.

As Shanks gambolled over to Satya's desk with his characteristic grin, Satya's sights remained fixed on the sports desk. The object of her attention however, remained unaware of her piercing gaze and was concentrating on his computer screen. With wide bright eyes, a nice broad smile and an aquiline nose in a youngish face crowned by hair that could be used in shampoo advertisements, Satya found it hard to look away. The more she stared, the more she believed that this person she was looking at had to be one of the most good looking men she had seen in real life. Also he was dressed in the way she liked men to dress, in a sober sky blue coloured formal shirt teamed up with a pair of worn looking classic jeans.

'Perfect!' Her mind trilled. It took a sharp elbowing from Rati for Satya to realize that Shanks was actually saying something to her.

'Ow! Oh sorry Shanks! Umm… I still have brain freeze after landing during Delhi winters after Kerala…I'm babbling… sorry! What were you saying Shanks?'

Shanks was unfazed by Satya's flustered reply. Come to think of it, nothing ever seemed to faze Shanks. He was busy digging into the packet of banana chips.

'Chill dude! I was just saying that I love these chips. Is there more of this stuff? It's just super delicious man!' He said while stuffing his mouth with chips.

'Oh ya, ya. Take as much as you want! I have more,' Satya replied and gave him the entire packet as she shuffled her feet, embarrassed at having been caught staring at the attractive stranger. At this point, Rati decided to speak up and take the same sort of initiative that Satya had shown in hers and Aniket's case.

'Um, Shanks, do you want to call the new guy over as well? We would have called him over, but we've not spoken to him or anything and we don't even know his name, so...um… why don't you?'

Shanks continued to relish the chips and replied in his usual laidback style, 'Who? Ayush? Ya, sure, cool will call him over'

Continuing to clutch at the chips packet with one hand, Shanks waved at Ayush with the other. 'Yo, dude! Ayush, come here man! They have awesome banana chips,' he yelled out. As Ayush strode towards the desk, flashing what seemed to be teeth worthy of advertisements too, Satya suddenly found it hard to look up.

'Hey guys,' Ayush greeted them in a pleasant boyish voice.

'And his voice is divine too,' Satya thought to herself, feeling more and more like she was in high school as each minute passed. Shanks pointed out at the group with a couple of fingers, which had a chip snugly fitted between them,

'Guys meet Ayush Narayan! Ayush meet Aniket, Rati, Rehaan and Satya. Oh and check out these chips man. Satya brought the chips! They are fantastic. I could just finish entire packets of it!'

At that, Aniket glared at Shanks, whom he now saw as a strong rival for the chips. But Shanks munched on blissfully unaware of the hate waves making their way to him. Meanwhile ignorant of the banana chip undercurrents, Ayush smiled winningly at all of them and took a couple of chips, 'Actually, I am watching my diet. So I can't have a lot. But thanks all the same. So, are all of you on the general desk or are you reporters?'

Aniket who seemed happy at Ayush not being yet another competitor as far as the banana chips were concerned, replied, 'Rati, me and Satya are on the general desk. We work on the actual production of the bulletins from the news reports to the tickers. But

Rehaan is on the business desk. He also reports from time to time. So you've just joined us? We noticed that you are with the sports desk.'

Ayush responded with gusto, 'Yup, part of the sports desk, but I won't be doing any production. I've joined as a Sports correspondent, as a reporter, nothing to do with production'

Ayush's emphasis on having nothing to do with production made Aniket wrinkle his brow and look as if he did not like what Ayush was implying. Rati, who seemed to sense Aniket's mood change, laid a hand on his arm as if warning him from speaking out. Satya however, had absolutely no complaints with what she was hearing and definitely none, with what she was seeing.

'Oh, so he must have work experience as well. Or else he wouldn't be a reporter at this age. Good looking and smart! That is so rare in our industry! What the hell! That is so rare anywhere!'

Satya thought, with a dreamy expression on her face. Rati too was smiling at Ayush in an admiring fashion, despite her restraining hand on Aniket. Weirdly enough, the only other person, who seemed to share Aniket's misgivings about Ayush, was Rehaan. He was looking at him wrinkling his nose in distaste. His earlier enthusiasm about the newbie seemed to have vanished into thin air now that he had actually met and talked to him. But he seemed to be reserving his judgement for now.

'Satya, if you're free, please work on this report on drunken driving on the increase in our cities,' Debashree called out from the copy editors desk. Wrenching her eyes away from the vision that was Ayush and making a moue with her mouth, Satya walked off to work. No one in the newsroom knew the state of her heart at the moment!

By the middle of the week, Satya felt like the vacation had taken place light years ago. It was almost like she had never been away from the chaos of it all. She was back in the afternoon shift and had fallen back into her schedule without a hitch. It was a Wednesday and she was on headlines duty today. This meant that she had to re-edit all the headlines and the teasers for all the reports that were on every live bulletin. Though editing a headline took only about five minutes, headline duty was still exhausting as it meant editing headlines for five main stories and four teasers for the reports that came up after the break every half an hour. And sometimes when the bulletins used the same stories over and over again, it was a challenge to make sure that new shots from the same one and a half minute story were used for the twenty-second headline each time.

Though it had been a particularly draining day, Satya was enjoying the feeling of being kept on her toes. Most of the reports playing today were well shot and it was not a pain going through the same shots again and again. Though a weekday, the channel had a two-hour special on Indian festivals and celebrations and that meant that Satya had gotten a two-hour break. She headed down to the cafeteria to grab a coffee. She decided to take the stairs instead of the elevator, because it was only two flights down and she thought that she needed to work off the couple of kilos she had gained thanks to her mother's pampering. She decided to text Rati to ask her to join her and if not, whether she wanted anything. As she reached the verandah by the first floor landing though, she slowed her steps. This was the landing where all the smokers headed to during their coffee breaks for a smoke and stopped for a few minutes to complain about the office, away from the newsroom cameras. As she wrinkled her nose at the heavy smell of smoke in the air, she heard someone yelling.

'How can you be so cheap? Just because I bum a cigarette off you, doesn't make it ok for you to talk to me like this!'

It was Ramyashri, one of the assistant producers. She sounded outraged. Satya did not know whether to walk past nonchalantly or wait till Ramya and whoever she was talking to walked away.

'Bloody ass!' Ramya swore vehemently.

'Ok that does it. I'll just sit on the stairs and wait it out,' Satya decided as her curiosity got the better of her. She sat down and listened, reasoning to herself that if it had been a private quarrel, the duo would have gone to a slightly more private place.

'Come on Ramya lighten up!'

It was a drawl that seemed so fake and so lascivious that Satya felt her skin crawl. She would have known the owner of that voice anywhere. It was Aneesh Ramnath, the desk head of her nightmares. He went on, 'So you wear a tight t-shirt and I tell you that it shows off your curves and that it fits you very snugly so? It's a compliment babe. You have a full body and I like what I see'

He seemed totally unconcerned about Ramya's yelling. He made it sound like him hitting on her was something Remya should take as a compliment. Satya's hand was itching to give him a slap when she heard the resounding sound of one echoing from the landing.

'That's to teach you some respect Aneesh. And if this hasn't done the trick, I'll just have a word with Nandan. Maybe he has a few others up his sleeve.'

Ramya's voice echoed sounding like steel. Almost immediately, Satya heard footsteps coming up. She froze not sure whether she should make a run for it or stay there and pretend as if she had not heard a thing. But there was no time for decisions. Suddenly she was looking up at Ramya who was standing in front of her with rage still written across her face.

'You heard?' she asked Satya.

Satya debated shaking her head for a split second before nodding and saying, 'Yup.'

Ramya shrugged, looking unconcerned and said. 'Well, then just pass along how the dumb ass got well and truly slapped by me. The more people know of his humiliation, the less people he will try it on.'

Satya wanted to applaud, but Ramya had walked on. Satya waited for two more minutes, before she continued to head downstairs. Aneesh was standing there with his hand to his cheek, looking out stubbornly. He turned at Satya's footsteps, probably expecting Ramya to have returned with Nandan. But seeing only Satya there, he let out an almost inaudible sigh of relief and turned away again. Satya ignored him and walked on.

The sights she had seen in her months here were insane. She had never imagined journalists behind the scenes or otherwise behaving this way. Satya had always been an idealist at heart. Before coming to

NOIDA, she had held the broadcast news industry in great esteem. She had imagined the men and women working here to be honourable, trustworthy people who would uphold ideals that are meant to be upheld. But her work and work place had taught her otherwise. There were incompetent people here as well as corrupt ones, the work shirkers and the ones who had made their way up because of their famous friends. The infamous casting couch of the film world was rumoured to have made its way to the world of TV news as well. Satya was disgusted by what she had just witnessed, because it only confirmed that sleaze had tainted the news world that she had always considered above reproach. She felt a knot in her stomach.

She ordered a hot chocolate and tried to console herself by arguing that sleazeballs made their way to every walk of life and she could not possibly pass judgement on the industry on that basis. The hot chocolate warmed her up, but as she made her way back to the newsroom, ready to tell Rati about what she had just seen, she still felt a little revolted. As she opened the door to the staircase, she balked and took the elevator up to the newsroom instead.

'He is so fake! I don't know how you cannot see it! Plus he looks down on production and production assistants! It's really very clear. Aniket saw it too! He told me so!'

Rehaan was saying, as he and Satya had their weekly Chinese dinner, which had become a ritual of sorts. Satya looked up.

'What? What did Aniket see? When? I was the only one on the staircase! And he never mentioned that he was there! He must have seen something else!' she said with an air of finality. Rehaan looked at her with a puzzled expression.

'What are you talking about?' he asked looking thoroughly confused.

'The same thing you are talking about! Aneesh and his slimy ways! What's wrong with you Rehaan? Secretly drinking or something?' she said as she waved her fork at him.

'Eh? Aneesh? Why would I want to discuss that slimeball who has nothing to do with our lives! I'm talking about Ayush, you nutcase!' he said, waving his fork back at her.

'Ohhh! Ayush! I thought you meant Aneesh! One minute, one minute, why do you think Ayush is fake?' Satya said with a slight frown.

'Something about him,' Rehaan mumbled like a sulky child who was being quizzed on his dismal report card.

Satya concentrated on her Hong Kong noodles and pretended to ignore his tone. Rehaan had been acting like this for a couple of weeks now and she was getting tired of his unreasonable disapproval. Ayush had exchanged numbers with the four of them, after the first introduction. And then he had done something that had made Satya's heart do a joyous skip. He had sent Satya a text message in the evening, thanking her for the chips. An elated Satya had messaged a lame "thank you" in response, following it up with a "how are you liking the office?" message, only to keep the conversation flowing. Ayush had replied and they had continued exchanging pleasant nothings for around half an hour.

Rehaan however, had not seemed happy about the turn of events at all. He insisted that Ayush was putting up an act and seemed hollow inside. But Satya refused to see things his way and brushed him off, saying he was paranoid. She also felt privately that Rehaan was just worried, that her liking a guy meant a potential reduction in the time Satya spent with him. But she did not let Rehaan onto what she thought. She knew he would not like it. The Chinese dinner was just her way of trying to put him at ease. This time it was Rehaan who was picking at his food and sulking. Satya knew that he was pouting. This was seriously not the way she had the envisaged the evening to pass. She really wanted to cheer him up. She decided to try a new tack.

'Oh, c'mon Rehaan! You're just sulking because you think he's cute and he's obviously not gay! It's ok baba! You'll find someone too! After all, you do have a year to search right?' She teased her friend. But Rehaan looked like he had serious misgivings about Ayush. He was in no mood for banter.

'No, that's not it Satya! Don't be irritating ok?'

He only called her Satya when he was truly annoyed. But this time Satya thought his qualms were misplaced. She would just have to give him time to get over it. But that did not mean that she could let her best friend put a dampener over the cutest thing that had happened to her in a while. And this after she had gone all out to make sure that he was OK. Satya decided to do some plain speaking with him.

'Listen Rehaan, I like him and would like to meet him over a coffee or so. And that's it for now. But the thing is, that you should not have a problem with that. Your opinion is important to me, but this time somehow I just have a good feeling about this guy. Plus, I never judge you for the people you are attracted to, so I think you should get over this. And be mature about it. And also eat your chilly chicken!'

She abruptly finished what suddenly seemed like a speech to her, and looked at Rehaan to gauge his reaction.

Rehaan shrugged his shoulders and said with a resigned expression, 'Fine, whatever you want. Though, I think you should be focusing on getting the reporting profile you wanted, rather than flirting with people of no consequence. Have you started sending the bosses mails like I told you to?'

Satya did not know whether to call him out in his avoidance of the issue or to be grateful that he had changed the subject. To keep peace with her best friend, she decided to choose to be grateful. She nodded and replied, 'Actually yes, despite the weekend, I managed to send them a comment on this pollution story that came in from Chennai and an environmental story from Kolkata. Basically I wrote comments about the camera work, the scripting and the way the sign off piece was shot. I also sent them a story idea on how the cattle catchers in Delhi are being shot by an international travel channel and how there is a group protesting against it saying that the documentary will showcase the poor side of India. They'd rather that the documentary be on 'India shining than India mooing'. Anyway, no replies so far, but I'll continue with it' Satya said. Rehaan smiled at Satya's way of putting it but did not comment.

Satya carefully wrapped noodles over her fork and said, 'Oh and I forgot to tell you. It slipped my mind with all this… Ayu... I mean Aneesh and Ramya business. Anyway, I met this guy called Karan Srivastava at the wedding reception. Devayani's husband's friend… He works for the Indian State in Bangalore. He's an assistant editor there on the Nation page. And like proper journos, irrespective of the wedding setting we are in, we started discussing news, what makes the headlines today, are bulletins more of TV shows? You know, usual media stuff. We ended up talking about the differences and the similarities in print and TV and at the end of it, he asked me to send him my resume. Do you think I should? I mean, I've never thought of print as an option.'

Rehaan looked thoroughly taken aback. He seemed to have completely forgotten that he was supposed to be sulking about the Ayush affair. Instead he looked aghast at what Satya had spoken about casually.

'Are you planning to quit? Tya, we just started here! And that too from TV to print? From Delhi to Bangalore? Are you sure?' he asked, shaking his head in disbelief.

'No, of course not! I mean… I don't know. I've not thought about it… yet. And it wasn't like it was an offer or anything. He just told me to stay in touch and send my resume, that's all,' Satya explained.

'Hmm. In that case, ya, you should send your resume and of course, it's always great to have journalist contacts in other cities.' Rehaan replied, looking extremely relieved.

'Right, so it's okay to have journalist contacts in other cities, just not on other desks, right?' Satya teased him.

'Oh! Stop it Tya! Date him if you want, but I reserve the right to say I-told-you-so!' Rehaan smiled back at her as he started shovelling his food in at top speed again.

It was three weeks into November. Monkey caps and sweaters, thick gloves and bulky inner wear and people huddling next to the coffee machine, for at least a measure of heat. These were just some of the common scenes in the newsroom. Satya had been sending out critiquing mails on reports and story ideas for two weeks now. Addressed to Nandan, Kedia and Padma, the silence from the head trio had begun to seem deafening. While Padma would call Satya over and assign her work on the shift, not a word was exchanged on her mails. Satya had not expected Nandan to respond, as he was too high up in the hierarchy. And as for Kedia, he had recently yelled at Tina when she had approached him with much the same request she had put across to Padma, a few weeks ago.

'You eh? Reporter? No experience! Not even old enough to be mature and telling me that you want to be a reporter eh?'

And so on and so forth Kedia had spewed, till a tearful Tina had backed away. After Tina's public dressing down, Satya was not ready to cross his path just yet. And so her mails continued with no response from any quarter. The good news however was that she was sufficiently distracted from the lack of response, thanks to Ayush. The text messaging was almost constant now and they had finally decided to meet up for dinner. Satya had swapped shifts with Rati who was in the morning shift, to get the evening off to get ready. She had made an appointment with the neighbourhood beauty parlour and headed there straight after work. She had decided to pull out all stops for this one.

Relaxed after a fruit facial and a head massage, Satya took her own time to get ready for her first date in two years.

'Today we will have our first proper conversation'

Satya thought to herself as she brushed her hair one last time, while she waited for Ayush to come and pick her up. Dressed in her favourite pair of jeans and a brand new orange sweater top, she thought she was appropriately clothed for what she hoped would be the first date of many. Her phone buzzed. It was a missed call from Ayush. It meant that he was already at the gate.

Satya took a last look at the mirror, picked up her new handbag, locked up and headed downstairs. And there he was, looking impossibly handsome, on his bike. She wished she had a camera so that she could click a quick photograph. She knew whipping out her mobile phone and asking him to pose would be too corny to do, so she just took her time looking at him to imprint the sight in her memory. For a person who normally winced at saccharine sweet romances and hated the corny stuff, Satya was not sure whether she felt happy about the way she was feeling right now. But the sight of Ayush seemed to make her want to deal with those feelings of doubt later.

He smiled at her and said, 'Ready to go? I was thinking we could head to McDonalds. I love the fries there. And I spent an extra hour in the gym so that I could eat properly.'

'Well, at least that's non-corny and unromantic and so my overdeveloped sense of cringing to sweetness can stay silent now!' thought Satya, who said out loud, 'Sounds great!'

She climbed onto the bike. As she leaned forward to tell him about how excited she was that they could finally talk face-to face, Ayush wore his helmet and started the bike to a loud roar. Satya ignored the irony.

'Well, maybe I should wait till we get there,' Satya thought, squashing the doubts that had tried to raise their heads again.

Satya could not stop shivering. And it was in no way due to the thrill of riding on a bike with Ayush. It had been much too cold to take a bike ride and her hair was now standing up in what looked like shock waves. And that too, like the ones cartoon characters sported when they pushed their fingers into faulty electrical sockets. By the time, they reached McDonalds, which was technically only a short ride away from her house Satya felt like her nose had fallen off. Her face was now icy and she had lost all feeling everywhere, especially her nose. Her hands were frozen despite the woollen gloves she had worn. It took her the supreme amount of determination she had to make the date work, to paste a smile on her face and walk in. If this had been a lesser male specimen, Satya would have invented an excuse and turned on her heel then and there. But this was Ayush and he deserved another chance. As she followed him into the burger joint, she sincerely hoped the meal would be happier than the ride had been.

They were twenty minutes into the date and apart from random chat about movies, music and TV shows, the conversation had not gone anywhere. Satya's intellectual nerve was yet to be tickled. Satya did not have a lot of inputs to offer on Ayush's love of wrestling, so she decided to wrest the talk to work. After all, it was what she had perceived as his quick rise to a reporters profile that had been one of his attractions in the first place.

'So what do you want to focus on as a sports reporter?' she asked as she sipped her drink. Ayush was gnawing on a French fry.

He stopped and said, 'Any sports. Anything. Cricket, football… Anything.'

'Okay…' She said, waiting for him to elaborate. When she saw there was no reply forthcoming, she continued, 'But what do you want to focus on really? Like what's your specialty?'

He had finished the fry and now started on another. The persistent rat like motion had started to annoy her. She had also noticed that apart from his gym routine, he did not seem to have a lot to say on anything else. He was looking less and less attractive by the second and it had nothing to do with his looks.

Ayush replied, 'I don't know. Just sports in general.'

His vagueness puzzled Satya. She was curious now.

'Where did you work before joining here? What beat were you on?'

'Oh, I was just interning at India twenty-four. I have never worked before. This is my first job,' he replied casually.

Satya pursed her lips. She knew that she would regret asking the next question, but she needed to know more.

'So how did you get to be employed by N.E.W.S India?'

Ayush breezily replied, 'Oh through Kedia uncle. He's my dad's friend. So dad told him I was looking for a chance to be on TV, because I need the exposure. You see, I want to be an actor later on. And TV is the best way to get exposure, right! Plus I've played cricket in school, so that ways I can report it also. So he told me to come over and here I am.'

Satya finished the rest of the meal in stony silence.

The next day, dressed in her most comfortable and oldest sweater and pair of jeans, she was sending out yet another story idea to the head trio, when Rehaan came to her desk with a steaming hot cup of cappuccino. He silently held it out to her as she pressed the 'send' button on her email. She took the cup wordlessly and took a sip shrugged her shoulders in apparent indifference and said, 'Say it! I know you're dying to!'

Rehaan burst out with obvious relief, 'I told you he was fake! I just knew it from the first time I laid eyes on him. I mean, I agree the guy was unbelievably good looking. Unfortunate that he didn't measure up when he opened his mouth though. Anyway, all's well that ends well!'

Rehaan had patiently listened to Satya when she had called him after the date and given him the entire story. But the good friend that he had always been, he had refrained from commenting or teasing Satya. But Satya had known that he would not be able to hold his silence forever. She knew that she would have done the same if she were in his place.

Satya made a face and said, 'Ya, ya, you're right. Weirdly, I think I wasn't even that into him. It was just a humongous crush, you know. He's nothing beyond a pretty face. His extent of intelligent conversation is limited to text messages. Anyway, moving on like we say in the bulletins, what's annoying me is Kedia! He is such a hypocrite! Here we are, trained reporters being used for production, when wannabe actors like Ayush, waltz in and start delivering lives on-air! I mean, what is that! How is that fair! This is supposed to be a news channel, right? Not some acting school for wannabes!'

Rehaan took a look at Satya's furious face, looked around the newsroom and said, 'Ok, now's not the time Tya! And definitely not the place…we will discuss this later. I need to get back to my desk now. Relax, ok? I promise we'll talk about this later!'

With that he hurried off. Satya took a deep breath, to calm herself down and went back to checking her mail. There was no response from the triumvirate. However there was one new mail. It was from Karan Srivastava from the Indian State.

"Dear Satya,

I had forwarded your resume to my boss, the editor-in chief here, after a discussion I had with her about you. We were wondering if you would be interested in working as a Reporter with us here, for the Bangalore bureau. If yes, do let me know, so that I can arrange for a telephonic discussion between you and her.

Waiting to hear from you,

Warm regards,

Karan"

Satya read and re-read the mail. Was this a sign? Was print reporting her destiny? Was it time to call it quits in the TV news industry?

12
SURVIVOR

Despite herself, Satya found herself waiting to hear from Karan Srivastava and his boss again. She had mailed him back, saying that she was interested in reporting from Bangalore and that she was open to a talk. Karan had seemingly jumped to it and within a week she had been on a call with the editor-in-chief of the Indian State. It had been a long telephonic interview. They had quizzed her about her educational qualifications, her reporting preferences, the work she already did. But what she had liked most of all, was the tone in which the interview had been conducted. She had been treated as a journalist and a professional, someone whose opinion counted. At the end of the forty-minute interview, she had hung up, feeling respected, confident yet confused. They had wrapped up on a positive note, telling her she would hear from them soon. But the thing was, that while she felt good about the interview, she was not sure about how she would respond to a job offer. It was December. In less than two months, she would have completed a year at N.E.W.S India. It was the interview with the Indian State however, that had made her feel better about choosing to become a journalist than she had felt in ages.

For eleven months now, Satya had locked away her dreams of being a developmental journalist. She had tried to immerse herself behind the scenes, hoping that the recognition for her work would be a transfer to the reporters' desk. Far from the recognition she deserved, Satya had not even gotten appreciated for the long and dedicated hours she put in. She was not even sure that anyone was watching her work anymore. It was just everyday stuff expected of, from every other news trainee or desk editor. And now the Indian State had reminded her why she had first thought of becoming a reporter.

Images of the impoverished villages who needed their plight to catch the media eye ... unfulfilled political promises about water and local schools... the unmet development goals that the nation needed... Stories waiting to be told! She had pushed them into the background waiting for that lucky break as a reporter, unwilling, but then she had no other option. And now, all those reasons came rushing back, clamouring for attention. Satya had not felt this good about wanting to be a journalist, since her first day here. The last straw had been seeing Ayush on air, with absolutely no training or experience, when she and her friends had continued to struggle on the desks.

This was not anything like the journalism classes back in college. No one had told them that they would be recruited as news trainees, who would be made to carry coffee for journalism graduates from other colleges. At N.E.W.S. India, they had been denied reporting assignments on no certain or uncertain grounds. They had been condemned to production, which was not high on their list of things to do in life. Satya personally, had been judged on the basis of her looks, asked to spice up tragic news, made to feel like the fungus at the bottom of the barrel and finally ignored totally. She had been mailing Nandan, Kedia and Padma for three weeks now and had not received a single response.

However, even with all that, Satya was still unsure about quitting and moving to print journalism. She had dreamt of being a TV reporter for so long, she was not sure whether it was right to give up on it after a mere ten months. On the other hand, moving to a renowned newspaper as a reporter would at least establish her credentials as a reporter and help her to update her resume. It would be a definite step forward as opposed to cleaning up other people's botched up reports, like she was doing at the N.E.W.S India desk.

Accepting the Indian State offer would mean leaving NOIDA and relocating lock, stock and barrel to Bangalore. Nearer home, in the same city as Radhika and best of all, away from the city that wasn't a city, NOIDA. Yet if she moved to print, how long would it take her to get back to the broadcasting industry again? Would she be branded a print reporter and someone unable to take the pressure of the TV news world? After all N.EW.S India was the best at the moment and once she resigned from the best, would she ever be able to walk back? There were too many questions to be answered.

Satya's head was aching. She had been having a mental tug of war ever since the interview. She had even gone so far as to list the pros and cons between the two options she now had in front of her. And though the pros list was completely in favour of the Indian State, she was still far from making a decision at the moment. It was a classic brain vs. heart case. Neither seemed to be budging an inch on the issue. Satya did not know what she would do if and when the offer letter came in from the newspaper. She had a sneaky feeling that it was highly improbable that an offer letter would not come her way.

A troubled Satya headed towards office. Rati and Aniket were in the morning shift and just leaving office as she reached. She had not told them the news yet and decided to delay it for a little while more. The two of them, herself and Rehaan had grown really close and she figured there was no point upsetting these two, without any concrete reason. She met them in the lobby and hurriedly rushed away, after telling them a white lie about having to meet the HR guys about an attendance issue.

Rati did not seem convinced, but Aniket was pulling her away, waving cinema tickets in her face. She took a last look at Satya's disappearing back, pulled her thick shawl tightly around herself and walked out in the bitter Delhi cold holding onto Aniket's hand. She decided to check up on Satya later.

Satya waved her electronic access card in front of the sensor absentmindedly. She barely noticed the door open to let her in as her mind ticked furiously.

'Please let there be a response from either Nandan or Padma. Or even Kedia! Please a response, any response. I will need to make up my mind soon. Please a response!' Satya thought anxiously. She could not think of anything else as she walked towards her workstation, past the edit suites and faces that were regulars on TV. The very faces that had seemed glamorous and unapproachable on her first day, were now friends and people she had shared workspaces or a coffee with. The edit suites and voice over machines were no longer just shiny pieces of the news beast, they were bigger cogs in the news wheel she was a part of.

'We could all quit and these machines would continue to stay on ... upgraded and maintained. These machines are worth more to the channel than me,' she thought. Her step faltered. She tried to focus on the positive and walked on to her workstation, willing it to have a positive response. She dumped her bag on the desk. She had pasted printouts of photographs next to her machine. As the computer whirred into life, she glanced at the snapshots of her life at N.E.W.S India.

There had been special moments sprinkled over the course of the year that she had spent here. There was one in which Aniket had wrapped Rati, Rehaan and herself in a bear hug. Another in the office canteen, with her face smeared with birthday cake and a number of desk editors surrounding her. Some ten of them dressed up in flashy Indian costume as they made their way to the Navratri party. Rati and herself having coffee in sector eighteen, the entire newsroom smiling at the camera at the channel's first year anniversary party. She closed her eyes.

There were also the times when a camera was not around to capture the joys and the triumphs of being a part of N.E.W.S India. The first time she had heard her voice on air. The first time a news anchor had mentioned her name on air. Nandan sending out a mail saying that the news flashes had been well handled, the day she was on the ticker. The high of withdrawing her first salary, no matter what the amount was. There had indeed been some good times. But they had been mostly with the people at work, not work itself. As in, these were not the moments that she had envisioned as her successes as a student of journalism. She cared deeply about the people she worked with. She knew that she had made some friends that would last her a lifetime, here at N.E.W.S India. But the question was whether she wanted to stay back for the friendships, while her career languished? Didn't friendships survive the test of distance? Or was she being too objective and unemotional? What was the right decision?

Satya's inbox flashed on the screen with a muted beep, alerting her to a new mail, jolting her out of her exhausting flurry of thoughts. Satya took a deep breath. Mentally and physically crossing her fingers, she focused on her inbox. Out of the hundreds of desk related mails that had come in, Satya's eyes instantly fell upon one particular mail. Her heart leapt. It was not the one that she had been wanting to see in her inbox though. There was no time to dilly-dally or debate anymore. Like the popular cliché, it was time to do or die. It was time for the final decision.

Satya waited for a lull in the news flow. She walked up to Padma who did not look very busy, as she sipped her coffee and leaned back in her chair. It had been an average day as far as news was concerned. No breaking news and just the usual politician speak as well as the one-odd crime story. Satya gritted her teeth and walked up to her boss and mentor in many senses of the word. The strangeness of the situation made Satya lose the usual awkwardness she felt with Padma. Usually while speaking to her, Satya had always felt as if words were stuck in her throat and that it would take a few umms and ahs for them to come out. Today, the situation had cured Satya of her nervousness. The words flowed out as if on their own accord.

'Padma, can I please talk to you in private?' Satya asked in a gentle but firm voice.

Padma looked up at Satya. She looked Satya over calmly and tilted her head to one side as if she was considering something. It was like Padma too had sensed a change in Satya's demeanour.

'Yes, of course!' she replied briskly and got up from her desk. They walked a few steps away from the general desk and stood in a relatively isolated corner. The newsroom TVs blabbered on in the background. Satya now thought of them as the soundtrack to her work life.

'So, what's on your mind? What is it that you want to talk to me about Satya?' Padma asked levelly.

'I just wanted to know whether you've been receiving my mails Padma. I mean I have been mailing you consistently with story ideas for a while now and there has been absolutely no response. I wanted to get a response of some sort from you. And I figured that I might as well ask you about it directly.' Satya said, looking Padma in the eye. It was Padma who was humming and hawing this time. She looked away.

'Umm, yes we have been receiving your mails. And we think it's great that you understand reporting the way you do. Very good, of course... but... Umm, we also think, that you are great on the desk... so...'

Padma trailed off and looked pointedly at her watch, as if to imply that she had no more time, for this particular conversation. However, Satya was not ready to give up so easily.

'So Padma, does this mean, that I have no option of moving out of the desk? Not even if my inclination lies elsewhere?' she persisted.

Padma was not ready for Satya's blunt questioning. She pursed her lips, tapped her watch and started to walk back towards her workstation. She paused mid way though and turned.

'I can tell you this Satya. I would not like you to leave the team. But this is not up to me anyway. Only Ram can answer your questions.'

Satya felt that substituting 'God' where Padma had said 'Ram' was probably a better option for the answers she was looking for. As Padma turned back to her work, Satya knew that there was no hope of support from her. Padma cared about her team far too much to let it suffer because a well-oiled cog wanted to leave. Satya went back to her desk and took a long look at the mail that had bolstered her courage to be direct with Padma, once and for all. She read it again. She would need as much mental ammunition as possible to deal with Kedia. And the mail from the Indian State gave her just that.

It proved that a media organisation was ready to take her on as a reporter. This was irrespective of her age, notwithstanding her lack of professional reporting experience. And this was certainly not because of the way she looked or because her parents had friends in the organisation. She deserved to know why N.E.W.S India would not give her that opportunity despite the way she had put aside her aspirations and worked for them. And there was only one way to find out. It was time to meet the man who had crushed her dreams ten months ago.

As Satya walked towards Kedia's cabin, she was conscious of how different she felt since the first time she had met him there. She remembered walking through the newsroom with steps that were shaky with excitement and quite a bit of nervousness. She remembered Rehaan knocking on Kedia's door and herself speaking up and then waiting for Kedia to assign them to beats. Then the man had passed what had seemed like a death sentence to Satya and her friends. It was true that over the months she had grown to appreciate the people who dedicated their lives to working behind the scenes in television news. But she also knew that it was not for her.

Though it had been less than a year ago, she knew that she had grown as a TV news professional in ways that she had never imagined. She no longer looked at news channels as the temples of journalism that she had once imagined them to be. She knew that in a half an hour bulletin, only seventeen minutes were devoted to the news. The rest of the time was pedalled to various commercial organisations, so that they in turn could peddle their wares on live television. Advertisements were as much the lifeblood of a news channel as the news reports were. She had learnt that a human tragedy without the spice of special effects and music would never make it on air. Tears on their own were worth nothing in the world of twenty-four hour drama. But she also knew that no matter how gruesome the story that opened the bulletin was, the bulletin always closed with a feel good story, which was inspiring and motivating. It was as if the channel was trying to tell the viewer that there was always hope and like many a Bollywood film theme, till something good happened, the show was not over. That was what Satya was hoping and wishing for. She wanted her 'happily ever after' to start. She did not want her time at N.E.W.S India to be over just yet. Satya knew that despite all its idiosyncrasies, TV was where her heart was and that today she needed to fight for her dream.

Kedia was in his office when Satya knocked. He waved her inside and gestured her to sit down. He took his own sweet time to talk to her, as he checked what seemed to be an inordinate number of messages on his phone.

He finally looked up and said, 'So how can I help you, eh? Padma told me, that you might come to meet me.'

Satya was not sure whether he was feigning ignorance or seriously did not know, what she wanted to meet him about. She decided to be as blunt with him as she had been with Padma.

'Sir, I want to know whether there is any chance that I can shift out from the general desk to reporting. I have been trying to open this conversation with you for weeks now and there has been no response.'

Satya figured what his response would be even before she finished her sentence, from the way Kedia's expression changed. His air of indifference was replaced by one of complete antagonism.

Raising his eyebrows pointedly Kedia snarled, 'So, you think we have nothing better to do here, than sit and reply to your piddling little mails, eh? This is a twenty-four hour news network. We get thousands of mails. We don't have time to respond to every single one, eh! Especially ones of no consequence like yours!'

Clamping down on her temper, Satya replied calmly, 'Yes sir, I understand that you do not have the time to reply to mails. But what about my question? My passion lies in reporting and I wanted to know, if there is a possibility of getting shifted out from the desk.'

Kedia banged his fist on the table.

'This is the problem with your generation. Everything needs to be on fast forward mode eh! Just because you can edit marginally well and look decent, you want to be on TV. You want to be a celebrity, eh? Do you think we are running a modelling agency over here, eh? We believe in having seasoned reporters with experience. Not some two bit fresher who wants to wave to her family and friends under the pretext of being a reporter!' he finished venomously.

Satya shot back, 'Oh that's right, you would rather have wannabe actors who have played cricket in high school reporting for you. How could I possibly imagine that someone with a masters degree in journalism and an experience in reporting could get a reporter's position here, right sir?'

Kedia banged his fist on the table again, this time with more force. He looked like he was about to have a stroke.

He exploded, 'The decisions we take are none of your business, eh. If you want to make sure that you still have that two-bit desk editor or news trainee or whatever post, get out of here right now! Get out! You are not fit to report, not here, not anywhere else.'

Satya got up, and calmly said, 'If that's what you feel, then I have nothing else to say.'

She walked out with dignity and headed straight for her desk. Satya went through the rest of the shift as if nothing had happened. Padma kept her busy with report after report to work on. And Satya too, suppressed her feelings till she had the time to deal with them. At the end of her day, she had wrapped up her work and reached a decision. She decided it was time to go through with it. She sat down and typed out her resignation with steady hands.

"Dear Nandan, Padma and Ram Sir,

This is to inform you that I have been presented with an opportunity to work as a reporter with the Indian State in Bangalore.

Therefore, I am tendering my resignation as a news trainee with N.E.W.S India.

This was not an easy decision and it took a lot of consideration. However I have to decide in favour of moving towards some of my career and personal goals.

My experience with the channel has been very rewarding. I

appreciate having had the opportunity to work for such a fine company. I wish you and the organisation continued success.

Please accept my resignation and make necessary arrangements to relieve me at the earliest.

Thanking you

Sincerely.

Satyabhama Menon"

She went through the mail again and with a small sigh of regret sent it to the three people she had been mailing story ideas to, till just a day ago. Satya walked out of the newsroom and headed home in an office car, with a heavy heart. The show had not ended on a happy note this time. While she was happy that she had a job in hand and that she was moving closer to home and family, the fact that her dream was far from fulfilled, irked her. This was not the scenario she had envisioned for herself, when she had started out on this path. Her professors in college had never once talked about being placed as a news trainee and working behind the scenes. They had never spoken about verbal sparring with senior news editors. This was not the world that she wanted to be a part of.

Satya had spoken only to her family and Rehaan after mailing her resignation in. She had not wanted to speak to anyone else. In the face of her unhappiness, both her parents and Rehaan had sought to support her rather than debate with her on the wisdom of the move. Yet all their love and kind words had not raised Satya's spirits. She knew she would take time to heal. Breaking up with her boyfriend had been so much easier compared to this.

The next day as she headed for office, she knew that she had never felt this bad about walking back into the newsroom. But that was just what she had to do and there were no two ways about it. The sheen of the newsroom that had attracted and impressed her on the first day seemed dull and tarnished today. Her eyes were a dull red. She had not been able to stop the tears despite trying hard. It was as if all her stress of being a news trainee was flowing out. She opened her mail with absolutely no expectations, save an acknowledgement mail from Human Resources. And sure enough there was a mail, but it was not from HR. It was from Nandan and uncharacteristically addressed only to her.

"Satya,

Do meet me in my office whenever you come in,

Nandan"

Satya did not know whether to laugh or cry. She had dreamt of this day in college when Nandan would call or mail her exclusively and congratulate her on her amazing work. And now the dream had come true, in a perverse way. Of all the weird things that had happened to her, this one had taken the cake. Though she tried to convince herself that she was beyond caring, she still felt a twinge of nervousness as she got up to go meet her soon to be ex-boss. She smoothed down her Kurta, ran a hand through her hair and gulped down the apprehension she felt, before knocking on Nandan's cabin.

Meeting Nandan was always a good thing, irrespective of the circumstances. He was always a gentleman at least as far as the women in the office were concerned, which was also the reason why a lot of the women in the office suffered from a major crush on their charismatic managing editor. His manners were always impeccable. And even the fact that Satya had just given up on his channel did not seem to have affected his behaviour towards her. He got up as she entered and immediately kept his phone aside. With his light blue crumpled cotton shirt and his hair looking as if it had not seen a comb in weeks, he looked more like an absent minded college professor than an award winning journalist and news show host. He smiled at her as if to put her at ease and took a pen, and tapped it on a paper he had on the table.

'I have your resignation letter here with me Satya. You guys joined us in February. We have a week to go for the year to end. And you are already leaving us! Fed up of us so soon?'

The tone was questioning but not accusatory.

Satya swallowed her nervousness and spoke up, 'Sir… um… I mean, Nandan, working for you has been my dream and I understand what a great opportunity that this has been. But the kind of work that I have been doing here has been far from anything that I want to do. I have been sending out feelers to indicate that I would like to shift out from the desk. And there has been no response. I decided to go all out and ask Padma and Ram sir about it. And the response was far from favourable. So I am left with no other option…'

Satya left her sentence hanging as Nandan tapped on the table with the pen and looked at her. He looked at her searchingly and said, 'Well, you didn't come to me Satya. You could have come to me before you sent this resignation letter. Quitting is never a solution you know. How could you have supposed that I wouldn't have helped?'

Satya did not have a reply. Her mind was whirring.

'Was he saying that he would have shifted me out to the reporters desk? So this means he's been watching my work and reading my mails, right! Have I made a mistake?'

Doubt combined with regret was swirling through her mind.

Nandan continued, 'You must know that our reporters desk here is filled to capacity- political, city, business, entertainment and whichever ones we have. So it is out of the question here. And from your letter, I gather that you are shifting to Bangalore? And that too with a previous employers of mine?'At this point he smiled. Satya managed to smile back. She figured that he had just been rhetorical about meeting him.

She took a deep breath and replied, 'Yes Nandan. I know the city and the Indian State is offering me a city correspondent's post. And this is something that I know I want to do. Like you said, if there is no space here, there is no point in me waiting, is there?'

Much as she wanted to sound dignified, Satya could hear the faint desperation in her voice. She wanted him to tell her to reconsider, to stay back and that he would make space somehow.

Nandan nodded gravely and then held out his hand, 'It was great having you around in the newsroom, Satya. You are an asset to any organisation and we...'

As she got up to shake hands with him, and rudely cutting into the best appreciation, Satya had received at N.E.W.S India, Nandan's phone rang loudly. As Satya excused herself, she heard Nandan speak to someone about a report he wanted on the Vidarbha situation.

'It's over,' she thought. 'I am already yesterday's news.'

She was supposed to report to the Indian State in the first week of February. They had given her time to give a month's notice and to move to the garden city.

'Time enough for a clean break,' Karan had mailed.

But "a clean break" was precisely what eluded Satya. The break from N.E.W.S India seemed messy and somewhere in between the night shifts and the constant chaos of it all, Satya realised that she had fallen in love with the channel. Breaking up with an actual person seemed desirable to the situation she was in. While one can always avoid an ex, it would be hard to ignore the presence of a news channel that was now garnering maximum TRPs and holding a record for the most watched in the nation. She knew that wherever she went she was bound to see the N.E.W.S India logo whirling through as she flipped channels or the channel's signature music beaming out from television sets as she walked through malls. What would make it worse was the feeling that the relationship could have been much, much more meaningful if she had shown the patience to stick on or if the heads of the channel had decided to give her the profile and respect she deserved. Doubtless, this would be one of the messiest break ups that she had to deal with.

However at the moment, she had the rest of the shift to go through and there was Rati and Aniket to inform. She sent Rati a message, saying that she needed to meet them and talk to them and then set herself to the tasks of the day. The work seemed different today. She felt like she was emotionally attached to every visual she edited and script she rewrote. After all soon, this would become a thing of the past. In between work, she would check her mail, for a response from HR validating her resignation and starting the procedure to relieve her from her work. HR seemed to be taking its own sweet time and Satya knew that the entire team packed up at five in the evening, so there was no point waiting for it after that. She felt like Padma was avoiding her eyes as she moved through the newsroom, coordinating between production and rundown editors. She felt like she had already become an untouchable as far as the TV news world was concerned. She felt black clouds of depression wrap her in a tight embrace.

Distractedly Satya went about her work. Midway through the shift, news came in of an actor's hit and run case in Mumbai and work became chaotic and non-stop. Satya was forced out of her misery as she dealt with the footage that was streaming in. It was only at the end of the shift that Satya got time to check her mail again. She was not expecting a mail from HR and so was not really inclined to check her inbox. But she did anyway.

Bleary-eyed from the constant staring at edits and the sleeplessness of the past few nights, the mail did not register with Satya the first time around. It took her two scans up and down the inbox to figure that the mail from Nandan seemed to be addressed to her. She clicked it in a hurry and read through it. It had been sent to Padma and Kedia as well. She read it out again, this time aloud in a half whisper, just to make sure that she had not misunderstood its contents. Her phone rang shocking her with its loud ring tone.

It was Rati, 'Hey Satya! Sorry, I'd left the phone on silent and was watching a movie. I just saw your message when I took my phone to switch it back to loud! What's happening? Is everything ok?' she asked in a rush, her concern coming clearly through the line.

Satya was silent, unmindful of Rati's voice on the other end.

Rati repeated urgently, 'Satya? Are you there? What is it that you want to talk about? Are you ok?'

Satya suddenly realised that Rati was talking to her from the other end. She replied in a dreamy tone, as if she had just awakened from deep slumber.

'Yes...Everything's ok. And yes, I have news... Very good news in fact! I'm leaving Delhi... I'm going in February. I just got transferred to Bangalore as a correspondent for our channel...'

EPILOGUE
SEASON FINALE

'Satya, all packing done *Beta*? Need any help?'

Satya's landlord, called up to her. Satya looked down from her veranda, suddenly shaken out of her impromptu flashback.

'No, uncle! I am almost done. Plus my friends will be heading over here soon for the last minute stuff before the packers come. Thank you for offering to help out.' Satya called back at him.

She smiled at him and watched him waddle inside with packets filled with vegetables and treats for the obese dogs following him. As she turned to go back inside, Satya knew that the one-off encounters with her ever-pleasant landlord, were one of the many things that she would miss when she left. She would miss the noisy pigeons that had kept her out of her own kitchen. She would miss the gossipy maid who was always trying to ply her with news about that naughty *Sahabji* in B-21. The slow rides on the cycle rickshaws in winter afternoons and drinking piping hot tea in the middle of night shifts...

the delicious street *Momos* in sector eighteen and the roadside *Masala* corn vendors… the cheap movie tickets for early morning cinema shows and the typical North Indian flavour to her life here.

Satya knew that there would be plenty to think wistfully about when she left the city that was not a city. It was weird because when she had started her sojourn here, she had never once thought that anything associated with NOIDA would get under her skin. Funny how the city had grown on her despite her violent resistance to it! NOIDA had become like one of those relatives who everyone wants to avoid when they are around and yet are missed when they are absent.

Satya smiled and walked back to the cardboard boxes that were waiting for her attention. But before she got back to tending to them, she knew she had to read the letter again. She had taken a print out of Nandan's mail and though it was only a few weeks old, it had fast become a well-thumbed, worn-out looking piece of paper. She looked at the clock and figured that she had around twenty minutes more to relax before the packers arrived. She took out the letter again and read through it for the umpteenth time. She knew the words by heart, by now. But every time she read it, she could not stop the smile from spreading across her face, as it had the first time she had read it. Nandan had wiped away the bitterness she had felt towards N.E.W.S India with a single stroke. The simply written email had been addressed to Padma and Kedia as well.

"Dear Satya,

I know that I told you that we couldn't accommodate you in the

Delhi bureau. But the Bangalore Bureau is a different matter altogether. I've spoken to the Bangalore bureau head, Anjali and she is more than willing to take in a new reporter from February.

Ram – Please take care of the paperwork.

Padma – Please relieve her at least a week in advance, so that she can take time to set up her accommodation before she starts this new chapter in her career.

Satya, you didn't think that we would let you go that easy, did you? All the best and do well. We expect a lot from you.

Warm regards,

Nandan"

Satya had been dumbstruck at first and then ecstatic at the unexpected mail. She felt like she had been given a wild card entry back into a competition, which she thought she had lost. She had run back to Nandan's office to thank him, which he had brushed away in his characteristic style.

'Just prove us right with your work. And if you really want to thank someone, thank Padma. She's the one who convinced us that we couldn't afford to lose you. Just prove us right Satya. Do your best!'

Nandan smiled at her and walked off as if restoring someone's dreams was all just a day's work for him. Satya looked at him gratefully as he passed and then ran down to Padma's desk from his office. She skidded to a halt by Padma's seat. A bemused looking Padma looked up from her workstation and smiled at Satya.

'I take it that you got the news?' she said calmly in her inimitable style.

Satya nodded with enthusiasm. While she felt like hugging Padma, she knew that would be wildly inappropriate and was not sure that Padma would appreciate the show of emotion. So she settled for a wide smile and said, 'Thank you Padma. This means a lot to me!'

Padma smoothed her hair back and said, 'Like I have told you already, I'll be sorry to see you leave the team. You were one of our strongest players. But having someone like you on the field means that our team has a lot less cleaning up to do. So it's all for the best. Do well and make sure that we get all those exclusives in Bangalore' she said, as she reached out and touched Satya's hand. For someone who was known for never expressing any sort of sentiment, this pat was almost like getting hugged by Padma. Satya was touched far more than she had been by all the wordy sentimental displays that she had seen over the years. This was indeed heartfelt.

While most of the newsroom was happy for Satya, there was of course the one odd group who would not join in the celebrations. Notable amongst the grouchy faces was Tina. She did not understand why Satya was getting an opportunity like this, while she had been trying to impress on everyone that mattered, that she was the best of the lot. Annoyed and frustrated, she had decided to take a page out of Satya's book. She had gone ahead and submitted a resignation, which detailed her very many achievements and how her leaving would be a loss to N.E.W.S India. However, what she had not bargained for was the immediate reply from HR accepting her resignation and giving her a months notice to move on. It was Rati who told the rest of the general desk that she had overheard Padma tell Debashree that it was Tina's constant self-promotion that had led to this reaction. Predictably to save face, Tina had let it be known widely, that she had quit to take a year off and prepare for higher studies abroad. And as she whiled away her month's notice, her oft-repeated phrase became, "I don't think the Indian media is ready for me."

Not everyone was as bitter as Tina though. Ayush for example, proved to be a nice enough guy, despite the dumbness. Though he had confided to Shanks that he was not really sure why Satya had never wanted to go out with him again, he had still sent her a congratulatory text. Satya had found that very sweet and had mused yet again on why the Creator had been so unfair as to make him such a perfect male specimen minus the intelligence.

Satya had always felt bad about treating him the way she did, when all he had done was utilise an opportunity that his father had gotten him. In all fairness, how was he to know that she was a frustrated reporter forced to live the life of a maid in waiting, when she had never told him about it. She knew that she had taken out her anger at Kedia on poor Ayush. She had behaved badly by sending monosyllabic replies to his texts and barely acknowledging his presence in the newsroom. Granted that she had been hurting, but she knew that it was time to apologise. She met up with him in office and thanked him in person for the sweet message he had sent her.

'I'm sorry, I never responded properly to your messages Ayush. I was busy with work and wrapping up and stuff,' she had told him, when she intentionally ran into him in the newsroom. He had flashed his pearly whites at her and assured her that he completely understood. And just before she moved away, he held her wrist and confided, 'By the way, I got a call from Mr. Bhandarkar in Mumbai. He plans to make a movie on the news industry and guess who's going to have a significant part!' It was an amused Satya who had wished him the very best of luck before walking away.

Sunil and Vidya had been two of the happiest people for Satya apart from Rehaan, Rati and Aniket. They had gifted her a book with tips on weekend outings from Bangalore. Vidya was already making plans to not only visit but also and go on some of those weekend trips with her. Sunil was on his own happy high. He had, had good news from Padma too. Debashree had finally decided to go back to her calling and move back to print. True to her character, she had sent a general mail to the desk highlighting the shallowness of the broadcast news industry and the next day she was gone. Her leaving had opened up a position on the copywriter's desk and Padma had asked Sunil if he was interested. Sunil, of course had agreed readily.

'So then we make my farewell party your celebration party as well!' Satya had said excitedly as Sunil had given her the news.

'Done! As long as that doesn't mean that I have to pay!' Sunil had teased her when she had done a little jig with Vidya in the newsroom at his news.

'Here's to Satya!'

All of them had chanted in unison as they raised their coke glasses, toasting Satya's success. It was the night before her last afternoon shift at N.E.W.S India. They had all gathered at Satya's favourite restaurant Dragon Chinese. She would have it no other way. Her friends had wanted to pool in for an expensive dinner, but nothing epitomised her days in NOIDA as much as the Chinese food from Dragon Chinese and Satya had insisted that they meet there. In her mind, no other place would be as appropriate for a farewell.

The gang was composed of the usual suspects. Rehaan had organised the party with Aniket, Rati, Sunil and Vidya. Shanks had wanted to make it too, but had, had to stay back in office to work on a one-hour sports show and had called Satya earlier, promising to drop in on her in Bangalore whenever he was down south. Satya beamed at her friends around the table and raised her coke glass back at them.

'So last dinner with us behind the scenes folks? Let me be the first to ask you the question every TV reporter asks in their career no matter how much they try to avoid it. How does it feel Miss Reporter?' Aniket joked in his hearty voice as he spooned generous portions of fried rice onto his plate.

Rati squeezed his arm and said, 'So like you Ani, to put it that way, when just the other day, you were telling me that you'll miss having Satya around.' She winked at Satya.

'Awww, Aniket! So sweet ya! Damn, I'll miss you guys too!' Satya replied with genuine emotion.

'I never said anything…' Aniket mumbled through a full mouth, while giving Rati a mock glare.

As they started off on a mock quarrel, Satya rolled her eyes at Sunil and Vidya who had turned up with a cake in the shape of a TV camera as dessert. She glanced across at Rehaan who had been weirdly silent throughout the dinner. It took them three hours filled with Hong Kong chicken, fried rice, mushroom Manchurians and an assortment of other Indian - Chinese dishes and repeated refills of camera shaped cake for the gang to finally wrap up. The restaurant staff looked thoroughly relived when the noisy gang finally walked out with packets of leftovers. Except for Satya and Rehaan, all the others were in the morning shift and so they decided to call it a night. They all headed their separate ways after promising to meet Satya at her apartment in two days, when she was supposed to leave. Rehaan was going to drop Satya home before heading home himself.

They were riding back home in silence, on a cycle rickshaw. Satya could feel the cold piercing her through her thick swathes of shawls and sweaters. Even her high quality thermals seemed to be no match for the cold. She shivered and turned to Rehaan to check on him. He did not seem affected by the chilliness at all. He was sitting with crossed arms, staring out at the almost empty roads, watching the odd vehicle flash headlights in the darkness. He was oddly subdued. Satya gently tugged on his sleeve.

'What's up with you? Are you sulking or something?' she asked. Rehaan shrugged. Satya poked him with her gloved finger.

He shifted around uneasily and said, 'Don't be dumb Tya. It's just that ... I don't know ... I don't know when we'll take a ride like this again... or go to Chandni Chowk... Or make middle of the night calls ...and when we were eating dinner, I was thinking that Chinese has become such a part of my life since we've been friends... I am never going to be able to eat Chinese again without thinking of you...' he trailed off, looking miserable.

Satya felt her chest tightening. She put an arm around his shoulders and said, 'C'mon Rehaan! Its not like I'm leaving the country or anything! I'm just moving to Bangalore. It's very accessible by buses, trains, flights, and all sorts of transportation options you know! And seriously, apart from the distance, nothing else changes! The SMS rates are marginally different, but now my call limits have increased so I can always call you. And besides what are the office phones for, if not for abusing, right?'

Despite his long face, Rehaan let out a chuckle.

'Ya, why not! After all, its not like we haven't done that before!'

The duo continued giggling and chuckling on their ride home, attempting to laugh away the sadness that had welled up in both of them just a few moments ago.

Now down in the dumps friends were something Satya could deal with. What she could not get her head around though, was the phenomenon of so-called senior journalists who are supposed to be mentor-like in behaviour, turning vindictive instead. Satya was clearing her desk on her last day, when Kedia who was passing through the newsroom stopped by.

'So by bypassing me you finally managed to become a reporter, eh?'

Kedia half snarled at Satya. Satya stopped mid-way from taking off the photographs by her desk and faced him.

'Sir, I never bypassed you. I came to you before I sent out my resignation. I mailed you for almost three weeks before I came to you and from day one, I've been telling you that being a reporter is what I really want to be,' she replied.

Kedia however was in no mood for logic and reasoning.

'Don't give me inane excuses Satya. You think being a reporter is just about being a pretty face, eh? Well now that you've wheedled your way into reporting, lets see how you will fare, eh? After all it's we sitting in Delhi that will assign you the stories. So once you're out in the field, you'll see why it was a mistake to bypass me.'

And with that he stalked off without giving Satya a chance to reply. She shrugged and went back to taking down the photographs.

'That was weird! Though I don't think that's the last 'eh' I'll be hearing!' she thought, as she resumed clearing her desk of the knick-knacks she had accumulated there.

And now here she was in her apartment, stuffing those very knick-knacks into the labelled cardboard boxes around her. There was still quite a bit of stuffing to do and she was packing with all her concentration when suddenly her doorbell rang. She hurried over to the veranda to check if the packers had arrived and let out a sigh of relief at the sight she saw. Not only was the Sharma movers and Packers Van standing by her gate, but also at the gate were Aniket, Rati and Rehaan.

All of a sudden, her apartment was a hub of activity. There were people sitting on boxes that were filled to the brim, helping them shut, as others pasted masking tape all over them. There were people numbering boxes and repacking ones with the kind of deftness and precision that Satya would have never been able to achieve.

Rehaan was belting out orders to the movers telling them to be careful, almost tripping over the boxes himself in his attempt to be everywhere. Rati and Aniket were double-checking the address labels and listing the number of boxes. Every five minutes, Satya found herself stopping and taking a look at her friends who were doing everything possible to make this change as hassle free as it could be. She could feel her eyes moisten and a lump appear in her throat.

'I am going to miss these guys! So, so much! How can I even expect to find friends half as good as these in Bangalore? What will I do without them?' Satya thought. She was trying hard not to burst into tears. As she noticed Rati looking at her, she hastily brushed them away. Rati walked over to Satya and led her by her hand to the veranda.

'You want to let it out? It's ok, you know? Go ahead' she said, her voice washing over Satya like a soothing balm.

'No, its ok…' Satya said in a small voice and shook her head and then proceeded to burst into tears. She tried to speak through her sobs.

'I am going to miss you guys so much. I mean as much as I love the idea of moving to Bangalore… this… This is hard! Much, much harder than I thought it would be,' she said, as she fumbled for a handkerchief in her jeans pocket.

'We'll come for a visit, so can you and there are always the calls and the Internet…' Rati said as comfortingly as she could. She was trying hard to find reasons that would make Satya feel better. Satya found the attempt endearing.

She wiped her tears and said, 'You sound like me when I was trying to console Rehaan the other day. Its ok Rati...I'll be ok...'

Satya took a deep breath, cleared her throat and repeated, 'I'll be ok! And also... Thanks you guys... thank you ... for being you' she said with eyes that misted over again.

'What's happening here?' Aniket sounded suspicious. He had walked up from behind with Rehaan.

'All ok?' he asked looking at Rati.

Rati smiled and replied, ' Yup all ok. What's the scene inside?' she said changing the subject to save Satya from further scrutiny.

'Come and see for yourself,' Aniket quipped. Satya shot Rati a grateful glance as she followed her friends back into the sitting room. The four of them stepped back inside. Satya took a moment to take it in.

All the boxes had been loaded. The shelves and cupboards were bare. The bed stripped of its mattress. It was looking exactly the way it had when she had first moved in. Except for the windows. She had left the curtains on. The windows of her apartment were smaller in size than most apartment windows and it had been hard finding ready-made curtains. She had rummaged through every curtain and drapery shop in NOIDA and quite a few in Delhi, when she had finally seen the cutest drapes hanging in a store window.

Dark maroon cotton curtains with prints of elephants in the style of an ancient Indian mural.

One look at them and it was love at first sight. Satya knew that these were the ones that would make her apartment her home. The owner was only glad to sell them as they had been lying there for ages anyway. A quick dry cleaning later, they were gracing her apartment. She looked at them now, as they fluttered in the breeze. She would miss waking up and seeing the elephants wink at her as they flew up and down, moving to the rhythm of the wind. But she did not mind leaving them behind, as it was almost like she was leaving a piece of herself in the apartment. Just like she was leaving pieces of her heart behind with her friends. She moved back into the centre of the room and threw her arms wide open. She looked at her friends and said, 'Group hug?'

They all moved towards her in unison and held each other. Giggles masked the underlying despondency they all felt at Satya's imminent departure.

And suddenly, before they knew it, it was time to go. The Packers truck had been loaded with her belongings and double-checked. And now the taxi to take her to the airport had arrived as well. As her friends loaded the cab with her suitcases, Satya took one last walk around the apartment that she had grown to call her home. She walked out of the door, pulled the door shut and walked downstairs with a heavier step than she ever had before. She knocked on her landlord's door after patting the dogs that were lying on the doorstep. After a quick goodbye, she handed over the keys and walked to the gate where her friends were waiting.

'Ok, no more time for goodbyes! If you leave now, you wont have to rush through security.' Aniket said looking at his watch. Rati who was holding onto him knew that he did not want a prolonged goodbye precisely because he did not want his friends to see him tear up. She nodded her agreement. Rehaan who was riding with Satya to the airport was already inside the car. Satya hugged Rati and Aniket quickly and got into the car as well. As the car pulled out, the two of them were waving fiercely.

'Call me as soon as you land,' Rati was yelling out. Satya nodded, not trusting herself to speak. She kept looking at her friends and her house till the car turned the bend and hit the highway.

The journey to the airport was uneventful and for the most part silent. Rehaan and Satya were riding along in companionable silence. The only thing punctuating the silence during the ride, were the calls Satya got from people in the newsroom wishing her the best of luck, and from her family who were excited to get her closer home. Between the calls and the occasional sentences exchanged between Satya and Rehaan, the car rolled into the airport.

Rehaan jumped out and got a trolley for her luggage. The Indira Gandhi Airport was being renovated and visitors were not allowed inside the domestic terminal. Satya hugged Rehaan quickly and walked inside pushing her trolley. She knew that any further talk would only make her burst into tears. As she stood in the queue for the security check, she turned back and through misted over eyes, she could catch glimpses of Rehaan each time the sliding doors opened and closed. Resolutely wiping her eyes on the sleeve of the jacket, Satya moved on to the check-in counter.

The engines of the plane had started rumbling. Satya had a window seat. She was sucking on an orange candy, which she had thoughtfully brought with the foresight of the airline being a low cost one. The flight started off on a slow pace as it began its course on the runway. And suddenly it lifted itself off the ground. As it was an evening flight, the lights were already twinkling across the capital. Satya peered out at the city, which she no longer had to call home.

'Was this goodbye?' she wondered.

But then again, the more she looked at the power capital she had a sneaky suspicion that this, probably was not goodbye, quite yet. As the flight soared high, the clouds closed over her view of the city. She was flying closer and closer to her dream profile. Satya leaned back and opened the in-flight magazine that had articles and reports on the garden city. She had a week to go before she joined the Bangalore bureau as a correspondent. She had no doubt that there was much in store for her there. But no matter what it was, she was sure none of it would compare with what she had gone through as a news trainee. Nothing was more humbling than the travails of being the lowest of the low in a news channel.

But now she had left that life behind. She was a news trainee who had transformed into a reporter to be. Feeling like a caterpillar that was fast sprouting wings, she felt warm inside.

She smiled and mumbled softly to herself, 'Stay tuned Satya. After the break, there's a lot more coming up on the show.'